TAKEN FOR GRANTED

BY
CAROLINE ANDERSON

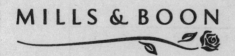
MILLS & BOON

All the characters in this book have no existence outside the imagination of the author, and have no relation whatsoever to anyone bearing the same name or names. They are not even distantly inspired by any individual known or unknown to the author, and all the incidents are pure invention.

MILLS & BOON, the Rose Device and LOVE ON CALL are trademarks of the publisher.
Harlequin Mills & Boon Limited,
Eton House, 18–24 Paradise Road, Richmond, Surrey TW9 1SR
This edition published by arrangement with
Harlequin Enterprises B.V.

© Caroline Anderson 1995

ISBN 0 263 79059 2

Set in 10 on 12 pt Linotron Times
03-9505-51474
Typeset in Great Britain by Centracet, Cambridge
Made and printed in Great Britain

CHAPTER ONE

'CAN I blow out the candles, Mummy?'

'No, stupid, it's her birthday—she has to blow out the candles. Can I have the first bit, Mum?'

'Maybe. And don't call your sister stupid, Ben.'

'Why not? She is.'

Sally set the cake down in the middle of the table, among the remains of the ham sandwiches and the apple and celery salad. A dollop of mayonnaise winked at her from her cuff as she pulled back her arm.

Great.

She would have to change.

'She isn't stupid, she's just younger than you,' Sally reasoned automatically as she dealt with the cuff. Damn, it was bound to mark.

'I want to light the candles now,' Molly said plaintively. It was past the eight-year-old's bedtime and she was beginning to whine, but they had to wait. . .

'When Daddy's home,' Sally told them.

'He'll be hours—he always is,' Ben said with all the pragmatism of a ten-year-old.

Molly's face puckered and she turned to her mother. 'Not always—is he, Mummy?'

She couldn't be bothered to argue with them—not tonight, on her thirty-ninth birthday. It was the last one she would celebrate for a long, long time.

Or she would if only Sam would come home.

She glanced at the clock on the oven, then at the

contents. Would the casserole survive if he was much longer?

The phone rang, and she picked it up.

'Hello? Sally Alexander.'

'Sally, it's Sam. I forgot to tell you, I've got a meeting tonight with a pharmaceutical rep. I'll be back late.'

She opened her mouth to tell him it was her birthday, but shut it again. What was the point? What was the point of any of it?

'Fine. I'll see you later,' she said heavily.

'Sally?'

She cradled the receiver with infinite care. It was that or smash it.

'Sorry, kids, Daddy's held up. He said go ahead without him.' She forced a bright smile and picked up the matches. 'Who wants to help me blow out the candles?'

The casserole looked unappetising. It was pheasant in red wine with tons of mushrooms and garlic—Sam's favourite.

She could freeze it, of course.

She couldn't be bothered. When would she heat it up? On another night when he would phone and say he couldn't make it?

She looked at the casserole, the sauce congealing, drying at the edges, and held it out at arm's length above the middle of the kitchen floor.

It smashed most satisfyingly.

It splashed her dress, of course, and the walls and the fronts of the cupboards.

She didn't care. The dress was already covered in mayonnaise and probably ruined, and anyway it didn't fit her any more.

She needed to diet. Having an extra slice of chocolate cake probably hadn't helped.

Still, she wouldn't be having dinner tonight.

She gave the carnage on the floor a cursory glance, and took the champagne out of the fridge. Crunching across the kitchen on the broken glass of the casserole dish, she retrieved a tumbler from the cupboard by the dishwasher, popped the cork and poured herself a hefty slug.

'Happy birthday, Sal,' she told herself, raising her glass.

'Thanks,' she replied, and drained the glass.

It tickled her nose. She poured another. That also tickled, and this time she giggled.

Damn him. How could he forget?

The laughter turned to tears, and she set the glass down and left the room, turning her back on the chaos.

She would sort it out tomorrow—if she was still here. It was by no means certain.

Sam shifted in his chair, bored. God, he hated these pharmaceutical 'sweeteners'. They had adjourned to a local Italian restaurant for 'a bite of something'. Sam was glad he wasn't picking up the tab. There were four of them: Sam; the rep; Martin Goody, the senior partner; and Steve Dalton, the other partner in the practice. Martin was divorced, Steve was still single, and there was no reason to suppose the rep was in a hurry to get home. He told endless stories about his exploits, and 'the wife' was constantly run into the ground. Sam didn't imagine for a moment that he would care if his wife worried about his lateness—if indeed she would.

Sally, on the other hand. . . He glanced at his watch. Quarter past ten—on the fifteenth of March.

Oh, God.

Sally's birthday.

He closed his eyes, a wave of guilt and remorse washing over him. How could he have forgotten?

'Sam? You OK?'

He opened his eyes again, and nodded. 'Yes—I'm fine. I'm sorry, I'm going to have to leave you—I've got a patient I'm a bit concerned about and it's preying on my mind,' he lied.

'Can't it keep for an hour?' Martin asked with a quick frown of puzzlement.

Sam felt guilty colour crawl up his neck. 'I think I'd be happier if I went now,' he said with absolute truth, and with another apology to the rep and to his bewildered colleagues he slid back his chair, retrieved his coat and left.

The drive home was agonising. What could he say that would make it any better? Nothing. He hadn't bought her anything, not even a card.

He called in at the all-night garage on the way and picked up an indifferent card and a box of chocolates. They weren't her favourite, but they didn't have any Belgian ones in the garage. Damn. He looked at the flowers, but they were tatty and bedraggled, definitely past their best. He walked past them, wrote the card in the car and then drove the last few miles home.

The house was in darkness, except for the light in the hall.

Damn, again.

Perhaps she was in the drawing-room at the rear of the house. He put the car in the garage and went in through the kitchen door, as usual, crossing the kitchen in the half-dark.

Something crunched under his feet.

'What on earth. . .?'

He stopped in his tracks and peered down at the floor.

Whatever it was smelt delicious.

He backtracked cautiously and flicked on the light. Something dark red, rich and with mushrooms floating in it—mushrooms and something larger—a pheasant?—and the remains of a casserole dish adorned the tiled floor and the front of the kitchen units.

An opened bottle of champagne—good champagne—stood on the side, an empty glass beside it, next to the massacred remnants of a chocolate cake. He studied the carnage in stunned silence, then, picking his way carefully over the mess, he kicked off his shoes at the doorway and walked into the hall in his socks.

'Sally?'

Silence, except for the ticking of the grandfather clock. The sitting-room was in darkness, but there was enough light to see that it was empty.

He crossed the hall and peered into the drawing-room. Darkness again. She must be upstairs.

He padded up silently in his socks, opened the door and went into their room. The bathroom light was on, and he could make out her form in the bed, hunched up in one corner.

She was mad with him. It showed in every line of her body. He sighed. He supposed she had every right to be, but she could have reminded him. Damn it, he was busy. She had nothing else to think about.

Self-righteous anger warred the guilt. Guilt won.

He sat carefully on the edge of the bed.

'Sally?'

'Go away.'

'Darling, I'm sorry.'

'It's not just the meal.'

'I know.' He put the chocolates and card under her hand. 'Happy birthday.'

She sat up slowly.

'You remembered.'

'Not in time. I really am sorry.'

'I should have reminded you,' she mumbled, 'only I wanted you to remember without being reminded.'

He nearly told her that she only had herself to blame, but he stopped himself just in time.

Instead he stripped off his tie, dropped his shoes and went into the dressing-room. He put his suit on the hanger, noting a mark on the lapel. Sally would have to take it to the cleaners for him.

He went back into the bedroom in his shirt and underwear, shedding them as he went, and slipped into bed beside her. He would win her round. He always could. It never failed.

I can't, she thought. I'm so angry with him, I can't be bothered to pretend to enjoy this any more, either for his ego or for mine.

He kissed her, his mouth warm and gentle. It made her want to cry. She used to love his kisses, but not any more. She had lost him, somewhere along the way, and this man was a stranger—a stranger who took her for granted.

She didn't want to be taken for granted any more.

So she lay there, without responding, and after a while he lifted his head.

'Oh, for God's sake, Sally, you've made your point,' he muttered. 'Come on.'

'No.'

'What?'

'I said no.'

He was still for a second, then rolled away. 'No?' he repeated, his voice incredulous.

As well he might be. She couldn't remember a time when she had refused him without a good reason—and not feeling like it didn't count.

'I have apologised for forgetting it was your birthday,' he went on. 'It's not as if I've been in bed with the rep, for heaven's sake!'

'I just don't feel like it,' she said, in a tone that brooked no further discussion.

Sam, however, was harder than that to deter.

'OK, let's have it,' he said heavily. 'Why not?'

Sally was fed up—fed up with being used, with being sweet-talked and cajoled and coaxed into forgetting what she was angry about. It wouldn't work this time, because she found the hurt went deeper than she cared to probe.

Hurt made her lash out, dredging up the truth.

'Because I find I can't be bothered to fake an enthusiastic response tonight.'

The silence was shattering. 'Fake?' he said softly, after an age.

She sighed and ran her hands through her hair. God, she must do something with it, it was a mess. A mousy mess. Yuck.

'What are you talking about?'

'Nothing,' she backtracked. 'I'm just being bitchy.'

'No, you're not. What did you mean?'

He wasn't going to let it go, she realised.

Hell. Her and her mouth. Why hadn't she kept quiet?

'I don't feel like it. I'm angry with you, and I just don't feel like pretending that I'm not.'

He flicked on the bedside light and sat up against his pillows.

'That isn't what you said,' he told her, his ice-blue eyes searching her face. 'That isn't what you meant.'

She turned away. 'How do you know what I meant? You don't know who the hell I am any more.'

There was silence, then he sighed heavily.

'No, maybe I don't. One thing's for sure—you aren't the woman I married.'

He flicked off the light, turned on his side away from her and thumped the pillow.

Sally felt the tears welling again. Was this all her protest would amount to? A huffy silence because she refused to sleep with him?

Her stomach rumbled.

God, she was starving.

It was sheer pride that prevented her from going and eating the supper off the kitchen floor—pride and the knowledge that it was by no means clean enough.

Instead she lay in the half-dark, staring at the broad expanse of his back, and wondered what on earth she could do that would give them both back the people they had married—the people they had loved.

Because one thing was certain. There wasn't much love lost between them at the moment, and if something didn't happen soon, it would be too late. . .

It was four days before the last of the casserole disappeared from the fronts of the kitchen cupboards.

The day after Sally's birthday, they all stepped

cautiously round the mess in the middle of the floor, the children regarding it with wide eyes but wisely saying nothing. By lunchtime leaving it there seemed such an empty protest that Sally dealt with it, functioning on autopilot while she pondered the state of her marriage.

Was it Sam's fault? she wondered as she scrubbed the red wine out of the grout between the tiles. Or hers?

Both?

God knows, she thought. Does it matter, so long as it changes?

But it couldn't change without help, and to help, they had to know what was wrong.

Defeated, she swabbed the floor down and gave up on the stains.

He was off that weekend, and on Saturday night Sally packed the children off to bed as early as she could get away with, and resolved to talk to Sam.

'There's casserole on the cupboard doors still,' he said as she came back into the kitchen. The table was still littered with plates, and he threw the remark over his shoulder as he disappeared towards the sitting-room with a glass of wine in one hand and the paper in the other.

'So clean it off,' she said sharply.

He stopped, turned and came back, his face wary.

'What?'

'You heard.'

'It isn't my job. I didn't chuck it on the floor. You clean it off.'

'No.'

He sighed and stabbed his fingers through his hair, tousling the gold strands still further. 'Look, Sally, for

God's sake, you've had days to deal with it. You've got nothing else to do——'

'What! Nothing else? How do you think your suit got to and from the cleaners? How do yo think the children get backwards and forwards to school? Who does the washing, the shopping, the gardening——?'

'It's winter, there's no gardening——'

'It's the middle of March, Sam—in case the fact has escaped you *again*. That's spring. I've been out in the garden for weeks battling the winter wreckage, pruning and clipping and weeding and tidying——'

'Aren't you lucky to have the time?'

Sally poured herself a glass of wine with a shaky hand. 'Oh, for God's sake, Sam—no, I'm not lucky! I'm bored out of my mind, I'm totally taken for granted—I'm wasted! I'm a lively, intelligent member of the human race, and I'm rotting in this——'

'If you dare call this house a hell-hole——'

'Yes? You'll what? Throw me out? I own half of it.'

'Only because of the crazy law in this country. I've put every penny into this place.'

'And I've just cleaned it.'

He looked pointedly at the cupboard fronts. 'On occasion.'

Her breath hissed out through clenched teeth. 'Bastard,' she said softly. 'You bought the house. It's me that's turned it into a home for us. Left up to you it would be a chaotic, empty shell.' She took a steadying gulp of the wine. 'It's so easy for you. You get up in the morning, you wash yourself, dress yourself, feed yourself, take yourself to work, do your job, come home, eat a meal prepared by someone else, pick up a drink and a paper bought by someone else and go and flop down in front of the television while the skivvy does another two hours in the kitchen clearing up after the chaos of the day and getting the children to bed!'

'Oh, yes, and during the day, of course, I've had nothing better to do than go off to garden centres and swan about at the health club and have coffee with friends and natter at the school gates—God, you women, you're all the same,' he ranted. 'You think you're so hard done by, and none of you have done a full day's work in years!'

Sally was so angry she could hardly speak. 'And who's got the weekend off?' she said finally. 'Who spent the afternoon dozing in the study? Who will spend tomorrow reading the Sunday papers?'

Sam gave an aggrieved sigh and shovelled his hand through his hair. 'So what? I work bloody hard, Sally. I deserve a rest.'

'So—do—I.'

He snorted, his eyes travelling round the kitchen. 'Well, it's a good job I'm more efficient at what I do than you are at what you do, or all my patients would be dead.'

Sally counted to ten. She was going to kill him. She was.

'Is medicine your chosen career?'

He looked a little stunned. 'Yes—of course. You know that.'

She nodded. 'Yes, I do. If you remember, that was how we met. I was a GP trainee, you were a junior partner. It was love at first sight. Seems a hell of a long time ago.'

She turned away, refilling her glass. '*I* chose medi-cine as *my* career as well—but I'm not doing it, Sam. Because of an accident of biology, I've had to turn into a cook, a gardener, a decorator and a financial manager.'

'Don't forget mother.'

'Oh, I don't—I never forget I'm a parent, but I think you do, very often. And a husband.'

'Well, I like that! I work damned hard to provide for you all, and what do I get in return?'

'A clean house, well run, a lovely garden to relax in if you were ever here, children who've been brought up to know the meaning of the word respect, a balanced diet to keep you fit while you go out there and slave your fingers to the bone in your *chosen career*. . .'

He had the grace to blush. 'Look, Sally, I've apologised. Give it a rest.'

'No, I won't—not until I've had my say. I didn't choose my lifestyle, and I don't like it. I feel frustrated, under-valued and worthless, and I hate that, Sam. I can't take it any more, and I won't!'

He set his glass down very carefully. 'What are you saying, Sally?'

He looked rattled. Did he think she was going to leave him?

Perhaps she was. She had no very clear idea.

'I just want—recognition.'

'Of what? Your cushy lifestyle? Give it a rest.'

'*My* cushy lifestyle? You haven't lifted a finger since Friday night!'

'And the last thing I had to do was admit a child to hospital with query meningitis!'

'Lucky you. The most important thing I've had to do in the last twenty-four hours is remember to put the chicken in the oven!'

'I don't know why you're complaining! You want for nothing—absolutely nothing. Anything you need, you have. Money, clothes, holidays—all you have to do is ask——'

'Exactly.' she met his eyes, her own burning like bright stars. 'All I ever have to do is ask. Maybe I don't *want* to have to ask you for money to buy you a birthday present! Did that ever occur to you?'

'Dear God, woman, you think you're so hard done by! What you need is a real day's work—that would soon shut you up! A short spell in the real world, just to show you how lucky you are.'

'Done!' She set her wine down and turned towards him. 'We'll swap jobs. You've got some leave owing to you—take it. Take three weeks. I'll do your locum, and you—you can put your feet up and do my job!'

The challenge vibrated in the air between them. Sally could feel the blood zinging in her veins. It had to work. He had to pick up the gauntlet.

'You're on,' he said softly. 'We'll start on Monday morning.'

She shook her head. 'Oh, no,' she said, just as softly. She picked up her wine and the evening paper. 'There's no time like the present—we'll start now.'

And with a smirk of victory, she walked past him and into the sitting-room.

He followed her. 'I wouldn't dream of leaving my desk covered in coffee-cups and clutter for someone else to take over. We'll start on Monday—and we'll spend tomorrow putting our mutual houses in order. I think that's only fair.'

He lifted the paper off her lap and walked calmly across the room, flicking off the television and switching on the CD player.

'I was watching that!'

He raised an eyebrow just the tiniest fraction. 'Were you? Before you do the dishwasher, or afterwards?'

It was all she could manage not to smash every single plate in the house.

Monday was one of those funny old spring days that was freezing to start with and by lunchtime was hot enough for a T-shirt. In a smart tailored suit that still—just—fitted, and tights and court shoes and a slip and all the paraphernalia of power dressing, Sally was boiling.

Boiling, and exhausted. She had hardly slept a wink for worrying about their rash exchange of jobs. What if she slipped up? What if she found she was so out of date that she couldn't tell an ingrowing toe-nail from a case of dysentery?

She had kept up, of course, out of interest—or so she hoped. But was reading all the professional journals that came into the house an adequate substitute for clinical practice?

Probably not. In three weeks, she could do an enormous amount of harm.

Then there was the reaction of the practice staff.

'Hello, Mrs Alexander,' the receptionist had sung when she went in.

The practice manager looked up and echoed the remark.

Sally shifted her bag from one hand to the other. 'Um—Dr Alexander, actually. Sam's Mrs Alexander for the next three weeks. We've swapped.'

Their jaws dropped.

'Swapped?' the practice manager said with a gasp. 'But—what about your insurance?'

'It's up to date, Mavis, it's fine.'

'But what about the payroll? What do I do about paying you?'

Sally smiled. 'That would be wonderful, of course, but in the circumstances I think we needn't bother with that. It would only go out of our joint account into our joint account.'

Mavis grappled with that for a moment, then tutted. 'It really is too bad of Dr Alexander not to have said anything. What about the patients?'

'What about them? He's on holiday, tell them. I'm doing his locum.'

Jackie, the receptionist, grinned. 'Mr Lucas'll hate that. He doesn't approve of working women. Tells me that every time he comes in, now he knows I've got children.'

He hadn't liked it, either. He had grumbled and complained the whole time she sounded his chest, and when she told him the only cure for his persistent bronchitis was to give up smoking he harumphed and stalked out, muttering about interfering busybodies and not knowing your place as he went.

The other patients were less overtly offensive, but she could tell that Sam's sudden defection was unwelcome.

'Don't get me wrong, dear,' one elderly lady said kindly. 'I'm sure you're a perfectly good doctor, but Dr Alexander has been so understanding and helpful about my condition—perhaps I'll wait and see him when he comes back. When is he coming back?'

'Three weeks,' Sally told her, and watched her face fall.

'Oh. Well, perhaps I'd better not wait. It's my dizzy spells, you see, dear. They seem to be getting worse.'

Sally took her blood-pressure, checked her history

and asked for a more accurate description of her 'dizzy spells'.

'Oh, my legs go all funny—I feel weak all over and then sometimes I just go down plop.'

'You fall?' Sally asked.

'Oh, yes, sometimes.'

'Do you pass out, do you think?'

She looked doubtful. 'I don't think so—no, dear, I'm sure I don't.'

'Could you do something for me, Mrs Wright? Could you walk over to the door and back for me, please?'

Sally watched as the woman did so, noticing that as she turned sharply she reached out for the doorknob, steadying herself for a moment before looking up with a shaky smile.

'Often happens like that, when I turn. Oh, dear. . .'

Sally helped her back to her chair, and watched as the woman removed her glasses and rubbed her eyes.

The glasses caught Sally's eye. They looked very modern in contrast to Mrs Wright's clothes, almost as if they didn't fit, or belonged to a different era. . .

Something clicked in Sally's memory. 'I don't suppose you've had new specs recently, have you?'

'New. . .? Well, I have, dear, actually, a few weeks ago. These are bifocals—vari-something, they're called. As a matter of fact they're a bit tight, so I only wear them on special occasions or if I can't make something out. Usually I wear my old ones.'

'I wonder,' Sally said thoughtfully. 'Did you ever have dizzy spells before you got the new glasses?'

'Before?' Mrs Wright thought for a moment. 'Well, now you come to mention it, I don't believe I did, not really. Only when I go to my sister's and we get the sherry out, but I don't suppose that counts, does it?'

Sally smiled. 'Probably not.'

Mrs Wright's face creased in worry. 'You don't suppose my eyes got worse because of something like a brain tumour, do you?'

Sally hastily reassured her. 'No, not at all. I think you may have had a different prescription, so your brain's having difficulty making sense of what it sees, especially with them being varifocals as well. It's quite a common reaction. Would you mind giving me the name of the optician? I'll ring them and find out if they've changed your prescription. Often if one eye changes more than another, that can cause dizziness.'

Mrs Wright fished in her bag and brought out a tatty old appointment card. Sally rang the number, asked about the prescription and then set the phone down with a smile.

'They've made the right eye much stronger. That could easily give you symptoms of dizziness at first.'

'So what do I do? I can't really see at all well now with the old ones, and to tell you the truth, I'm afraid to wear the new ones too much.'

'I think you should. Actually it's the chopping and changing that's confusing your brain, and if you stuck to the new ones, you'd probably find you were much better very quickly.'

'Well, if you say so, dear,' Mrs Wright said doubtfully. 'I could always try it.' She sounded highly sceptical, as if it couldn't possibly be so easy.

Sally crossed her fingers under the desk. 'I hope it works. Come back if not and we'll have a closer look, but I'm fairly confident that's the cause of your problems.'

Mrs Wright headed stiffly for the door, then turned

carefully to say goodbye. 'Shall I send in the next patient, dear?'

'If you would, please.'

The door closed, and Sally leant back, her teeth worrying her lip. What if she *was* wrong? What if it was something much more major and the glasses were just a distraction?

She didn't have time to worry. The next patient came in, and the next, and the next, and the temperature climbed steadily.

By the end of her surgery she was hot, bothered and ready for a nice, long shower. She hadn't had time this morning, because she'd been awake so much in the night that she'd slept through the alarm, and Sam, so used to her getting up and bringing early morning tea, had slept in as well.

Consequently there'd only been time for one of them to shower, and guess what?

She stuck her head round the door of the reception office. 'Anything urgent for me?' she asked.

The practice manager, Mavis, shook her head and continued her phone conversation with a patient.

'I'll be at home, then,' she told them, and headed for the door.

It was cooler outside, but she still felt sticky. It was nearly twelve. If she hurried she should still have time to shower and change into something more comfortable before going back for two.

Sam was in the garden when she arrived, and heaps of black bin-bags were stacked on the edge of the drive.

'What are you doing?' she asked.

'Scarifying the lawn. How did it go?'

'OK. What's for lunch?'

'Lunch? I don't know—what did you have in mind?'

She raised an eyebrow. 'What did I have in mind? How about coming home, having a plate put in one hand, a mug in the other and told to put my feet up?'

Sam snorted rudely. 'You're joking—I'm busy.'

'No you're not. We're swapping roles, remember? It was bad enough not getting early morning tea today, without having to forage for my lunch. Anyway, I want a shower. That should give you a few minutes to knock up something fascinating.'

Tossing him a cheeky grin, she turned on her heel and headed for the door.

'Sassy little mouth,' she heard from behind her, and the grin blossomed into a full-blown smile. This was definitely going to have its up-side.

At one-thirty the phone rang.

'Mrs Alexander, you forgot to sign the repeat prescriptions before you left. They're due out after two.'

Sally sighed. 'OK, Jackie, thanks. I'll be back in ten minutes.'

She gave her cup of coffee a regretful glance and stood up.

'Problems?'

She looked at Sam, sprawled comfortably on the sofa in the little sitting-room off the kitchen. Not for the world would she admit she had fouled up.

'Nothing I can't handle,' she said breezily and, picking up her bag, she headed out of the door.

The afternoon was busy, followed by a hectic evening surgery.

Mavis caught her on the way out of the door. 'Sam rang,' she told Sally. 'He said the car needed filling up and don't forget to do it or you'll run out.'

'Doesn't he trust me to do anything?' Sally muttered. She wondered how he'd got on with the children after school. Would he have sat them down and done their homework with them, or just let them watch telly? Well, she couldn't do everything. . .

She drove to the nearest garage, which happened to be where they'd bought the car, and pulled up beside the pumps. The filler cap was on the other side, of course.

Cursing mildly, she backed out, crashing the gears she had grown unused to, and pulled up on the other side of the pumps to fill the car.

The down-side, she reflected, was that Sam had the big automatic Mercedes estate, and she had his little Peugeot diesel runabout. More sensible for town work, easier for parking in little spaces and far more economical, but she wasn't used to it and frankly didn't want to be. She missed her luxuries.

The pump switched off, and she paid for the fuel and got back in the car. Nearly seven. She was starving. Lunch had been a bit hasty and seemed a long time ago. She wondered, as she crashed the gears again, what Sam had dreamed up for supper.

As she pulled away up the road, she became gradually more and more aware of the horrendous noise from the engine. Great clouds of black smoke poured out of the exhaust, and the engine was misfiring like a pig.

She pulled up immediately and switched off, staring in puzzlement in the rear-view mirror as the inky fog behind her sowly disappeared.

What ever could be wrong? She'd only just filled it up. . .

Oh, hell.

Furious with herself, anticipating Sam's initial anger and then the endless miles he would extract from the incident at dinner party after dinner party, she made her way back to the garage on foot.

Fortunately the service receptionist was still around, and managed to hide his amusement well. He gave her the keys of a courtesy car, asked her to sign the insurance form and promised to deal with Sam's car.

She drove home in a mixture of defensive anger and self-recrimination.

Sam greeted her on the drive. 'What the hell have you done with my car?' he said in amazement.

'I filled it up,' she said through gritted teeth.

'So?' Sam said patiently.

'With petrol.'

She closed her eyes and waited for the explosion.

CHAPTER TWO

THE silence was palpable—for as long as it lasted. Then Sam found his voice.

'WHAT?' he roared. 'How the bloody hell could you possibly do anything so *stupid*?'

'Easily. I never drive your car—I certainly never fill it up——'

'Perhaps that's just as well, if this is what you're going to do to it!' he ranted. 'Do you have any idea of what you've done, putting petrol in a diesel car?'

Sally sighed inwardly. This was going to be every bit as difficult and awkward as she had imagined. 'The mechanic did explain. He said all they have to do is flush out the fuel tank and rinse through the fuel lines——'

'If you haven't damaged the engine, which is quite likely. At the very least I expect you've wrecked the fuel injection pump and that'll be hundreds of pounds. I expect you drove it about four miles before you realised—had it overheated?'

Sally controlled her own temper with difficulty. 'I had driven about a hundred yards when I realised something was wrong. That's all. It'll hardly cost anything.'

Sam harumphed and stomped into the house. 'Well, you'd better be right, lady, because you're paying for it.'

'With what, dear Liza?' she called after him. 'My locum pay?'

The door slammed in her face.

With a sigh she opened the garage, put the courtesy car away and went into the house, to be greeted by the children in tears.

'What's wrong?' she asked, her motherly instincts roaring guiltily to the fore.

'Daddy threw out Molly's painting, and I tried to stop him and he pushed me out of the way and I hit my arm on the cupboard,' Ben told her, his chin wobbling.

'I did a picture for you,' Molly hiccuped, 'of a big shiny sun and a tree and a pony in a field and he said it looked like a pregnant camel anyway and he screwed it up and said it was bedtime. . .' Fresh tears spurted from Molly's eyes, and Sally scooped both children up against her chest and held them, washed with guilt and anger and remorse.

After a while they calmed down, and she took them upstairs, chivvied them gently through their bedtime routine and tucked them up.

By the time she got downstairs again she was exhausted, starving and wondering what on earth she'd let herself in for. Sam was standing in the utility-room, ironing a sheet of gaudy, crumpled paper.

'I'm sorry,' he said gruffly. 'I was so mad about the car. I shouldn't have taken it out on the kids. I'll go and apologise.'

'Forget it, they're asleep,' she advised him, studying Molly's crumpled painting with affection. Sam was right, the pony did look like a pregnant camel. 'What's for supper?' she asked.

He stabbed his hand through his hair, switched off the iron and sighed. 'There's some pizza left. I didn't get round to doing anything for us.'

Sally wrinkled her nose. Instant frozen pizza was

probably her least favourite meal—especially cold, left-over instant frozen pizza. 'I'll heat some soup,' she said tiredly.

'You need more than that. Do you fancy a take-away?'

'Can we afford it—with all that money we've got to spend on the car?' She couldn't keep the sarcasm out of her voice, and frankly she was too tired to try.

'I imagine the cost of a take-away is just a drop in the ocean by comparison,' he muttered.

'Look, Sam, I'm sorry about the car,' she said heavily. 'I didn't do it on purpose. I was tired, worrying about the children and thinking about a patient. The car really wasn't uppermost in my mind.'

He sighed. 'It's OK. We all do silly things from time to time. I'll go and pick something up.'

'Just make sure it's not a woman.'

He snorted. 'I haven't got the energy. In case you haven't noticed, I've been tackling the garden all day.'

'I noticed—I'm still hungry,' she said pointedly. 'It must be lovely to have time to play around in the garden on a nice sunny day like today.'

The tightened jaw and black look warned her off.

'Are you having a sense of humour failure, Sam?' she teased gently.

'Yes, I bloody well am,' he scowled, and, picking up the keys of the Mercedes, he stalked out of the door. 'Chinese or Indian?' he threw over his shoulder.

'Anything but pizza.'

The door slammed.

'So do you think it's feasible? Perhaps I should have sent her to the hospital for investigation. What if she's right—what if her failing eyesight is caused by something in her brain?'

'The optician would have picked it up. Sally, have faith,' Martin Goody said encouragingly. 'You're a good doctor. Trust your instincts.'

Sally sighed and drained her coffee-cup—the fourth that morning. 'OK. I'm sorry.'

Martin smiled. 'Don't apologise. It must be difficult coming back in without warning.'

She returned the smile weakly. 'Yes, well, I always was impulsive.'

Martin pursed his lips thoughtfully, then shot Sally a searching look. 'I know it's none of my business, but are things OK with you and Sam?'

She struggled between loyalty to Sam and honesty with his senior partner, her old trainer and their long-time friend. 'Ok-ish,' she said eventually.

'Only ish? Sounds worrying.'

She threaded her hands through her hair—still a mess. She must do something with it—and met Martin's searching honey-brown eyes. 'Yes. I think it is worrying. I've lost him, Martin. We had so much, and it's gone. I feel I don't know him any more. We used to have such fun together, but just recently. . .'

Martin reached over and squeezed her hand. 'Don't give up on him, Sally. Make him take stock, make him fight for what he wants. He loves you—he thinks the world of you and the children. He probably doesn't show it on a day-to-day basis, but God knows that's easy to let slip. I did, and look where it got me.'

He paused, his face sad. 'I didn't realise how much I'd lost until it was gone, but without Jane and the kids life's just an empty shell.' He met her eyes, and his were filled with lonelines and pain. 'Don't let your love slip away, Sally. Hang on to it. It's just too damn precious to lose. . .'

He stood up abruptly and left the room, his shoulders ramrod-straight.

Sally's heart went out to him. He had been divorced for three years now, and in all that time she had hardly ever seen him smile.

She swallowed hard. She couldn't let it happen with her own marriage. They had too much to let it go without a fight.

She had the first part of the afternoon off—she would use it to good effect. Reaching for the phone, she rang the hairdresser. If she had to fight to get Sam back, she needed every weapon in her armoury honed to perfection—starting with her hair.

Later that afternoon, after she had had her hair cut and some low-lights put in it to liven up the colour, she went back to take her evening surgery.

Her last patient was a woman of about her own age or slightly older, intelligent, educated but depressed.

'I think I need HRT,' Mrs Deakin told her. 'I'm tired, fed up and I've got no sex drive.'

Join the club, Sally thought to herself. 'Do you have a partner at the moment?' she asked, following up on the tired and fed up before the HRT.

The woman rolled her eyes. 'Of course. Ungrateful husband, ungrateful kids—I love them, but it's like a millstone.'

'Do you work?'

'Did you mean outside the home?'

Sally returned the wry smile. 'I did.'

'No. I suppose that's the trouble. No change of

scene. A friend of mine told me there's no aphrodisiac like a new lover. Maybe I should try it.'

Sally's smile faltered. Would she come to that with Sam? 'Interesting idea, but it's hard to reconcile with loyalty and fidelity, isn't it?' she said to Mrs Deakin.

'I was joking—I think.'

Sally twiddled her pen, thinking of Sam again. 'Perhaps you need to rediscover the old lover.'

'I thought HRT might help me do that.'

'Not if boredom is the only problem.' Sally questioned her about any menopausal symptoms, family history of thromboembolus, heart disease, hypertension and osteoporosis, and her own history of menstrual bleeding patterns, loss of libido and vaginal dryness.

'I'm not really dry—I'm just not interested.'

It was a symptom Sally recognised only too well. 'I could try you on HRT if I examine you and find no physical reason to exclude prescribing,' Sally told her, 'but I really wonder if your problems aren't as much emotional as physical. Can you take off your things and hop on the couch?'

While she examined her breasts and pelvis for any mass or abnormalities, Sally delved deeper into the history of her current problems. There didn't seem to be anything concrete, just a grumbling not-quite-rightness that was obviously distressing.

She picked up the woman's hand and looked at her nails. They looked fragile and brittle. Mrs Deakin told her it was a relatively new problem.

'Are you having any night sweats or flushes?'

She shrugged. 'Well—yes, but I thought that was just the heating being on at night over the winter. My hair seems to be dry and uncooperative, too—I wish it would look like yours.'

Sally laughed. 'I've just had it done—it looked like yours this morning. Perhaps you just need to spoil yourself a bit.'

Mrs Deakin shook her head. 'It's more than that. I just feel I'm falling apart.'

While the woman dressed Sally tapped the computer buttons and called up the HRT drugs available to her. 'Look, I don't think you're bad, but I want to try you on patches. The hormone's gentle, there isn't too much of it and it could be what you need to make all the difference. Come back and see me in a fortnight, OK?'

She handed the woman her prescription, and as she rose to leave, Sally gave her another piece of advice. 'Get your hair done. It won't change anything, but you'll be amazed at how much better you feel about yourself.'

'That sounds a bit autobiographical.'

Sally grinned. 'I wonder why?'

The woman left, and Sally shut down her computer and made her way to the reception office.

'Anything for me before I go home?'

'The garage rang—your car's ready.'

'Oh. Right. Thanks.'

Sally drove to the garage, swapped cars and paid the—amazingly—very reasonable bill, then headed home, hugely conscious of her lucky escape and desperately trying not to crash the gears.

There was no sign of Sam as she pulled in, and she put the car away and made her way into the house.

The kitchen was clean and tidy, the dishwasher humming in the background, and she could see something bubbling gently in the oven.

Voices drifted down from upstairs, high, happy children's voices and Sam's low rumble. As she crossed the hall she heard a giggle from Molly, and a splash, then Ben ran across the landing, stark-naked and dripping.

'Hi, Mum!' he yelled.

'Hi.' She went into the bathroom and found Sam perched on the edge of the bath making shampoo castles out of Molly's hair.

'Hello, Mummy,' Molly piped from under the bubbles, and Sam stood up and kissed her cheek.

'Hello, darlings. Good day?' she asked.

'Not bad.' Sam eyed her thoughtfully, then gave a low whistle. 'You've had your hair done.'

She suppressed the smile. 'It needed it.'

'You look lovely. Why don't you go and get a drink and I'll rinse Molly off and get her into bed. I'll be down soon.'

Oddly, she felt excluded. She trailed into the bedroom to the sound of Molly's laughter, changed into old jeans and comfy slippers and went down to the kitchen.

There was a bottle of wine breathing on the side, and she helped herself, sipping it thoughtfully. Sam was very well-organised tonight. Perhaps he was feeling guilty about last night—or maybe the message had got through.

Her palms felt suddenly clammy. What if he tried to make love to her? She wasn't sure she felt ready for that yet. They still had too much baggage in the way, too many years of neglect and indifference to get out of the way first.

She heard his footsteps behind her, and a large, warm hand cupped her shoulder. 'Why don't you go and kiss the kids goodnight and then come back down for supper?'

She nodded, flashing him a bright smile, and went upstairs. What was he up to?

She said goodnight to the children and went back down to the kitchen, to find Sam dishing up rice and chilli.

'Smells good,' she said, sniffing over his shoulder.

'It's a packet sauce, so it might be foul. Cooking isn't my forte.' He handed her the plate and headed for the table, clearly preoccupied.

'I'm sure it'll be lovely,' she told him, and ate it all, even though, as he said, the sauce was foul.

As soon as they had finished he whisked the plates away, poured her another glass of wine and held out his hand.

'Come into the drawing-room and put your feet up.'

'Not the sitting-room?'

'No. It's a bit chaotic still.'

She resisted the urge to glance in as they passed the door. She knew what she'd find. The kids could wreck a room in two seconds flat. Instead she allowed Sam to lead her into the drawing-room.

It was a chilly evening and the fire was lit, the logs hissing gently in the grate. It was very restful.

She allowed Sam to manoeuvre her on to one end of a sofa, and was unsurprised when he sat at the other end.

'Put your feet up,' he said softly, patting the cushion beside him, and she kicked off her slippers and turned round to face him, tucking her toes under his warm, solid thigh.

He studied her thoughtfully. 'You look lovely,' he said after a while. 'She's done your hair well.'

'Thank you.'

There was a flicker of something in his eyes. 'Don't thank me,' he said, and his voice had a husky quality that made her shiver. He looked away, running a straight, blunt finger round the rim of his glass.

'Sally, we need to talk.'

'Mmm.'

His breath hissed out on a sigh. 'The other night— your birthday. When I tried to make love to you and you said no.'

'I was tired and angry, Sam. You'd forgotten my birthday——'

'Is that all? I don't think so. I think this is about much more than you being tired and angry because I forgot your birthday. I think it's much deeper, and much more significant.'

She chewed her lip. She hated confrontations and so did Sam, but once he made his mind up, he could be worse than a terrier.

'You said something else, too.'

Sally had a sinking feeling in the pit of her stomach. She thought she'd got away with it, but clearly not.

'Something?' she said weakly.

'You said you couldn't be bothered to fake a response.'

She swallowed. 'I was mad with you. I didn't want to pretend I wasn't.'

'No, you said you couldn't be bothered to fake a response *tonight*—as if you had before, in the past.' He turned his head and met her eyes searchingly. He looked threatened, and she hated what she was about to do to him. If only he'd give up, but that wasn't Sam's style.

'Had you?' he persisted. 'Faked your response?'

The words seemed about to choke him. Sally looked away, unable to hold his eyes. 'Yes,' she said softly.

Above her toes she felt his thigh twitch, as if he'd flinched. Guilt tore at her, but he was relentless.

'When?'

She shrugged slightly. 'I'm not sure exactly. The first time. . .'

'First time?'

She looked back at him. 'The first time.'

His eyes closed. 'Go on.'

'It was a couple of years ago, I suppose. I was tired, you'd changed our holiday dates without telling me and you were mad with me for booking a holiday at the wrong time.'

He groaned. 'Then.'

'Yes, then. You wanted to make love to me—or maybe you just thought you could win me round. I don't know. Anyway, I didn't want to be won round. I felt I had a right to be angry, and I wasn't going to give it up, but I couldn't argue any more and I couldn't face another confrontation with you.'

'So you faked.'

'Yes.'

'All of it?'

She nodded, and his breath hissed out sharply.

'You couldn't have done—I would have known.'

'You didn't,' she told him gently. 'You didn't have a clue. I made sure of that. The next time I felt guilty, and I wasn't angry, so it was easy to let you coax me into it.'

'Did you fake then?' he asked. His voice was scrapy, rusty-sounding.

'No. I didn't need to, then or for a while. Later, though, when you were busy at work and getting stroppy about things not being done—I felt used, unloved——'

'Unloved? Sally, for God's sake——'

'Unloved,' she repeated firmly. 'Used. Taken for granted. We'd had a row about something trivial, and when we went to bed you tried to make it up by making love to me. I didn't want another confrontation, so I just. . .'

'Faked again.'

'Yes.'

He swore softly and succinctly under his breath. 'And since then?'

'Off and on. Much more, recently.'

His jaw worked. 'When was the last time I made love to you that you really—that you didn't fake?'

She took a steadying breath. 'About a year ago.'

He swivelled towards her, his eyes incredulous. 'A year?' he whispered. 'Dear God, Sally.'

She stared down into her drink, perilously close to tears.

'Why? Why didn't you just tell me to go to hell? How could you let me use you like that?'

She swallowed. 'You weren't, not really. In many ways I was using you, cheating you. It was easier than talking about all the things that were wrong—easier than facing the fact that we might not have a marriage left.'

Her eyes slid shut, tears slipping down her cheeks.

The silence stretched endlessly.

'Is that a serious possibility?' he asked at last.

'I don't know. I just know I can't go on like this, being taken for granted.'

He took her glass out of her nerveless fingers and set it down, then reached for her.

She lay motionless in his arms, unable to respond. She felt so tired, so sad inside.

'Am I really that much of a brute?' he asked raggedly.

'You can be—when you're tired and you aren't thinking, you can be very hurtful.'

His hand smoothed her hair back away from her face, and he bent his head and kissed away the tears.

'I'm sorry. I love you, Sally,' he said gruffly. 'I may not show it, but I do love you.'

She couldn't say the words back to him. He was waiting, but her throat seized up and she couldn't make a sound.

'Sally? Do you hate me so much?'

She shook her head. 'No. I don't hate you, Sam, but I don't know if I love you any more.'

'Oh, Sally,' he said raggedly. 'That's a hell of a thing to say. Do you really feel so bad?'

'I don't know how I feel,' she told him truthfully.

His hand was hesitant, smoothing back her hair, his fingers trembling slightly.

'I'm sorry,' he whispered, and then his mouth touched hers, his lips feather-soft against hers. His kiss was gentle, persuasive, but she was too empty inside to respond.

He lifted his head. 'Sally?'

'No, Sam, please.'

'No?'

'No—please!'

He sighed and let her go. 'I don't want to force you. I only wanted to make it up to you.'

'I don't want to make love. Please. I really don't.' She straightened away from him. 'You do this every time, try and win me round by making love. If you weren't so damn good at it maybe we would have sorted out our problems years ago, instead of me allowing you to distract me and sidetrack me from the real problem.'

He looked genuinely puzzled. 'I'm not trying to sidetrack you, Sally. I know we need to sort our problems out, but for God's sake, this is a problem, too.'

'No, Sam, it's a symptom. For years we've treated the symptom and left the problem festering underneath, but it won't work any more. This needs sorting out properly, not just a quick cuddle to paper over the cracks.'

'I've never tried to paper over the cracks, Sally. I didn't even realise there were cracks. I just knew that very often the only way I could reach you was to make love to you.'

He took her hand. 'Sally?'

She turned and met his eyes, and the sadness in them hurt her tender heart.

'I need you,' he told her quietly. 'You're fundamental to my happiness—the only thing that stops me from going crazy.' His thumb grazed her skin absently. 'Don't leave me, Sally. Please. Don't go—not without giving me another chance.'

She pulled her hand away gently. 'Don't ask me to make promises I may not be able to keep,' she replied, her voice low. She picked up her glass and drained it, then stood up. 'I'm going to bed. I'm on duty tomorrow night, I'll need my sleep.'

'I'll come up in a minute.'

'OK.' She went, relieved to have a little space, but worried about Sam. He'd sounded so—lost, so sad.

She blinked away the tears and climbed wearily up to bed.

Please, God, let it all come right.

Sam watched her go, his heart choked with emotion. Slowly, bit by bit, he sorted the feelings out.

Shock, first and foremost. Shock and disbelief. He hadn't really expected her to promise not to leave him, but her reply—hell, it sounded as though she really felt she might go. Pain washed over him. Was he really so dense that he hadn't even *noticed* her unhappiness all these years?

Probably. Evidently he was so lousy and selfish a lover that he hadn't even noticed that her response was faked.

Faked.

God, that word hurt.

A year, she'd said. Hell. A whole year he had made love to her and she had just pretended, all of it, the warmth, the tender caresses—and the end, all those desperate little noises she made that drove him over the brink. . .

His gut clenched, desire ripping through him. Those noises had always finished him off, smashed through his control and left him helpless. She'd known that, of course. After twelve tumultuous years, she'd be well aware of her effect on him.

Frustration swamped him, sheer, unadulterated sexual frustration. He wanted her, needed her— needed her now, this minute, desperately. Not sex, but Sally, warm, willing, generous—the Sally he had fallen headlong in love with twelve years ago, the Sally he had married—the Sally he had used and abused and whose love he had all but destroyed.

He felt the desire ebb away. She was right. Whenever they had a row, he always tried to make love to her afterwards, but was it just to win her round, or because he couldn't bear to see those lovely soft green eyes filled with hurt and confusion? He had always tried to apologise the only way that came naturally. Did she really see it as papering over the cracks?

Sorrow. That was the last emotion, a huge, terrible sadness deep inside. Was their marriage really dead? Had he lost her?

Dear God, no. Please, no.

He stood up, sucking in his stomach. He could do with losing a few pounds, tightening up a little. Perhaps he'd join Sally's health club, go and work out a bit and tone up those muscles. Perhaps he'd jog a bit.

Perhaps that would help. And maybe, just maybe, he ought to follow her household routine and find out just how tedious and depressing it really was. He couldn't believe it was that bad, but she seemed to think so. He'd try doing it properly and see how it was, and let her have a fair crack at his job. This three-week stretch should do it.

Then, surely, she'd realise how lucky she was.

Please God.

What if she discovered she loved being back at work and decided she could live without him and the kids?

He swallowed a sudden lump in his throat.

No. She would never abandon the kids.

But him?

He swore, softly but comprehensively.

'You're going to have to come up with some pretty fancy footwork this time, Alexander,' he said softly, and, flicking off the lights, he followed Sally up the stairs to bed.

CHAPTER THREE

THE following day Sally didn't have time to think about their conversation. She was on duty from her morning surgery through till the following morning, and it was one of those days that seemed to bring illness out in spades.

Her surgery was unusually busy, but after it was finished she called on Sue Palmer, a pregnant woman who had phoned the surgery requesting a visit.

'I suppose I could have come to the surgery,' she said, 'but I felt so washed out—I hope you don't mind?'

'Of course not,' Sally assured her. 'What's the problem?'

'I just feel a bit tender low down on my tummy.'

'When's the baby due?' Sally asked, flicking through the notes.

'The end of April.'

'That makes you about thirty-five weeks?'

'Uh-huh.'

'And are you getting Braxton-Hicks contractions?'

'The little practice ones? All the time. Today, though, it all feels a bit more tense.'

Sally felt her abdomen but couldn't detect anything abnormal. 'Any blood loss?'

'No.'

'Problems with the waterworks? Smelly urine, pain when you pee, anything abnormal?'

She shook her head.

'Bowel problems?'

Again, she shook her head. 'Only the usual fight with constipation because of the iron pills. Why? Do you think it might be a grumbling appendix or something?'

Sally shook her head. 'It's possible but unlikely. No, I think you might be going into labour.'

The woman looked unsurprised. 'I thought I possibly was, but it seemed rather early.'

Sally laughed. 'Babies have a way of suiting themselves. Let me have a listen and see what I can hear.'

She took out the foetal stethoscope to listen to the baby's heartbeat and, bending over, she placed her ear to one end of the funnel-shaped instrument, the other end resting firmly against the mother's abdomen. After shifting the stethoscope a couple of times, she was able to pick up a lovely clear heartbeat.

She timed it at about a hundred and forty beats a minute, right in the middle of the normal range. The baby wriggled, and the heart-rate increased slightly, exactly as she would expect it to.

She straightened up with a smile.

'Well, he-she seems fine,' she said cheerfully. 'I think we'll keep an eye on you, though. Rest for what's left of the day, get your husband to cook you a meal tonight, and see how you are tomorrow. If you feel more tender, or if anything changes, then ring the surgery immediately, or even the hospital. We'd rather be on the safe side but I think you might just be trying to go in to labour a little early.'

'Will it matter?'

'At thirty-five weeks? No. The baby's almost fully developed now. There'd be no problem at all.'

She shut her bag with a snap and stood up.

'Remember: rest, plenty to drink and get your husband to do the running around.'

'He'll love that.'

Sally grinned. 'Do him good. Stay there, I'll let myself out.'

She finished her rounds and went home at two for lunch.

'You're late,' Sam said as he put a bowl of soup down in front of her. 'Busy morning?'

'Aren't they all?'

He smiled understandingly. 'Yes. Who've you been to see?'

She told him about the patients she had attended, and when she mentioned Sue Palmer his ears pricked up.

'Might be nothing, but I'd pop back later and check her if it was me.'

'Funny. I was thinking that. I don't know why, but I think I just have a bad feeling about her.'

'You could always admit her.'

'On what grounds? There's nothing obvious wrong, and not very much that's not obvious! She's just not feeling brilliant, but the baby seems fine. I don't know, perhaps I'm just being neurotic.'

'I don't think so. Get that soup down you before the phone rings again.'

She had almost finished when the mobile warbled gently. With a resigned sigh she switched it on.

'Dr Alexander.'

'Sally? It's Jackie. Two more calls have just come in, and one's your way. I thought you might like to go out and deal with it on your way home. It's a child with earache. I've checked the notes and there's no history.'

'Thanks, Jackie. I'll do it on my way in. What's the other one?'

'Someone with vomiting, but they're right by the surgery.'

'OK. I'll do the child, then come back to the surgery for the notes.'

She jotted down the details, then with a weary smile to Sam, she left.

He cleared away the soup bowls into the dishwasher, then checked his watch. Two-fifteen. There was just time to see about his exercise routine before he had to pick the kids up.

He drove the two miles to the country hotel where the leisure and fitness club was, and, slapping on his most winning smile, he approached the reception desk. There was a pretty girl perched behind the desk, small and dainty, her dark hair piled in tendrils on top of her head above wide grey eyes and moist, ruby-red lips. A badge pinned over her generous left breast announced that she was Amy, Fitness Instructor.

'Hello, there,' she said, her smile friendly, mildly assessing.

'Afternoon——' he leant forwards slightly and read her badge for effect '—Amy. I wonder if I could ask a favour?'

'Sure—ask away.'

'My name's Sam Alexander. You probably know Sally, my wife.'

'Oh, yes.' The girl straightened and eyed him with interest. 'How can I help you?'

'Uh—we've swapped roles for a while. She's doing my job, and I've got the kids, the coffee-mornings and

the gardening.' He grinned enticingly, and got a flatter-
ing response. Good. This was going to be a walkover.

'I just wondered, as Sally won't have time to come,
if we could swap membership for the next couple of
weeks—nothing official, but just let me use the gym
instead of Sally. I know it's irregular, but. . .'

He held her eyes, and the girl dithered most gratifyingly before crumbling. 'Oh, OK, just for the next
couple of weeks, though—and provided you don't tell
everyone. Do you want me to go over the equipment
with you?'

'Could you?'

She slid out from behind the desk and wiggled most
attractively through into the gym. He followed her,
burying his grin.

'Right, this is the Schwinn bike—it's a warm-up bike
that works on air resistance. I'll give you two minutes
on that before your five minutes of stretching——' she
made a quick note on a chart '—and then three groups
of ten at——' she eyed Sam thoughtfully '—forty kilos
to start on the chest-press. Know how to use it?'

Sam nodded. She went over the other equipment in
the same way, then got to the treadmill.

'Ever used one of these?'

He nodded again.

'It's easy to programme. Do you want to walk or
jog, and uphill or on the flat? You can programme in
an incline, or a set course that gives you a variety of
terrain and speeds.'

'Let's just go for jogging on the flat at first. What
does Sally do?'

'Sometimes the course, but usually she just does
thirty minutes on the flat at seven miles an hour.'

Sam was impressed. He hadn't realised she actually

worked hard at keeping fit. 'I'll—er—I'll do the same, I think. Perhaps a bit faster, as my legs are longer.'

The girl eyed him doubtfully. 'Are you aerobically fit?'

He laughed. 'Reasonably, I hope.'

'OK, well, try that and see how you get on, but any stress and just stop. Oh, and keep an eye on your heartbeat—there's a monitor over there that works on handgrip. The instructions are dead simple. Then five minutes of stretches again and wind down on the bike for another two.'

'Fine.'

He went to change, then came back and climbed on the bike. Great. No problem. He pedalled happily, the rev counter showing fifty-four revs a minute, and was very pleased with himself until a skinny little woman jumped on the bike beside his and he caught sight of her rev counter. Seventy-two? Good grief!

His time came to an end then, but he was due back on it at the end of his routine and he vowed to do better next time.

The weights were no problem. All the exercises that relied on power to weight ratio were easy for him, because he was and always had been very strong. Alternating upper and lower body exercises, he worked until he had completed the programme set for him.

Feeling disgustingly pleased with himself, he walked over to the treadmill. Thirty minutes at seven mph, eh? Well, he'd give it a whirl.

He started up the tread, pushing the speed up gradually until he broke into a run, then started the timer.

One minute—no problem. This was going to be a breeze.

Two minutes—was it his imagination or was it warmer today? He wiped his forehead against his shoulder, then concentrated on pacing himself. Longer strides, he thought.

Three minutes— a tenth of the way there. God.

He could feel his heart pounding, and the muscles in his thighs were beginning to scream. This was ridiculous. He'd soon get his second wind and he'd settle into the routine.

Four minutes. Hell's teeth. He could feel the sweat pouring off him, the T-shirt clinging to his back. He was breathing hard—no, he was panting like a hot dog in the sun, for God's sake, but he was damned if he was giving in. He'd hang on to the rail, get a bit of support.

No. No arm swing. Bad idea.

Five minutes yet? No. Four and a half only. Not even a sixth of the way. He swallowed, his mouth dry, and ran his tongue over his top lip, catching the beads of sweat.

Pain—his legs, his chest—got to keep on—got to keep going. . .

'I think you've had enough,' a voice said calmly in his ear, and suddenly, blissfully, the treadmill was slowing.

He stumbled to a halt and glared at Amy. 'I hadn't finished.'

'Yes, you had. Come on, Sam. Over here, let's check your heartbeat.'

He almost fell off the treadmill and followed her across the room. His legs felt like jelly, his heart was pounding like a steam-hammer and his lungs were screaming for air.

'Hold that firmly but not too hard.'

He fastened on to the grips like a lifeline, and she switched on the monitor. After a few seconds a number flashed on the screen.

'Hmm,' Amy said.

Sam was appalled. ' A hundred and ninety-two?'

'Rather high, Sam. I think you ought to start a little more gently, don't you?'

He nodded dumbly, shocked, and watched as his pulse slowly dropped to a hundred and fifty.

Amy ushered him out through a fire door into the fresh air, and brought him a paper cone filled with ice-cold water.

'Sip it,' she advised, and pushed him down on to a low wall.

He slumped over, elbows propped on his knees, and listened to the screaming in his body subside to a steady wail.

'You're going to hurt tomorrow,' Amy said.

Sam snorted. 'If I live that long. My God, I don't believe I'm that unfit!'

'When did you last exercise? And I don't count sex.'

He ignored her grin. 'Years ago.'

'Now how did I know that? You need to start gently after such a long lay-off. Why don't you go and lie in the spa bath for a while and ease those muscles? Then I'll work on a programme for you to do, starting tomorrow. If I can get you to a point where you and Sally can go for a run together a couple of times a week, then you should be able to maintain your fitness easily at home. But now. . .'

She ran her eyes over him, and this time he recognised the assessment for professional and not personal interest. If he hadn't already been scarlet from his workout, he would have blushed at his stupidity. Of course she wasn't interested in him.

Damn, he was forty-one, unfit, overweight—well, only slightly, perhaps, but enough to put *her* off—and although he still had all his hair, there was the odd touch of grey in the gold. What the hell would she see in him?

He gave her a grateful smile. 'Thanks for rescuing me from my stupidity.'

She grinned. 'My pleasure.'

'One thing—don't tell Sally. She'd kill me.'

Amy's smile widened. 'I'll see. Depends how well you behave yourself.'

'I'll be totally obedient,' he vowed.

He stood up, horrified to find he was already stiffening up. 'I'll go and lie in the spa,' he told Amy, and headed for the changing-rooms. God, he hurt. At least his heart had slowed down now. Only for Sally, he thought painfully. He wouldn't do it for anyone else in the world—not even himself. But he would do it for Sally.

Amy watched him go, tall, his head held high, shoulders square, hips lean and taut above those long, powerful legs. Give him a few days working out and he'd be fit again. It was only his aerobic fitness that was questionable. The rest of him—well!

He was too old for her, of course, and anyway he was married, but he was still unquestionably a very attractive man. In his youth he must have been a real heart-breaker. Even now, she thought, with those gorgeous blue eyes and that very sexy smile. . .

She'd enjoyed flirting with him. Little games helped to pass the time. She glanced at her watch. Only one hour to go and she could go home. She'd phone Rick when she got in. There was a film she wanted to see, and then later. . .

Sue Palmer's condition hadn't changed when Sally checked on her before evening surgery. She was still slightly tender, but there was no evidence of contractions. Appendicitis was looking more likely, but Sally didn't want to jump the gun, and the baby seemed well enough, with a good steady heartbeat.

Giving strict instructions to phone her with any change, she went back to the surgery. The waiting-room was crowded—surprise, surprise, she thought.

She went into Sam's consulting-room and flicked through the notes quickly, but there was no point in delaying the issue. She pressed the button to call for the first patient, and settled down to a hectic couple of hours.

Towards the end of her surgery David Jones, a man in his late forties, came in looking very uncomfortable.

He sat down in front of Sally, his left hand wrapped round the right side of his ribcage, and told her he was in pain.

'It started a couple of days ago—well, it had been a bit sensitive on the skin for a day or so before that, but now—well, Doctor, the pain! Right in the ribs, like they're on fire or something.'

Sally asked him to remove his shirt, and he did so with extreme caution. There was nothing to see, and nothing to hear with the stethoscope. 'Have you had a cold recently? Any other virus?'

He shook his head.

'How about the rest of the family?' Sally asked, carefully inspecting the skin over the painful area.

'No, we're all well really. At least, now we are. My daughter got divorced last year and that knocked us all back a bit, but other than that we've all been fine.'

'What a shame,' Sally said sympathetically.

'Yes. Terrible, what with the kids and all. Still, she seems to be coping now.'

'Any back trouble at any time?' she asked, wondering if there was a possibility of intercostal neuralgia from a trapped nerve in his thoracic spine, but she thought it unlikely.

'No, I never had any back trouble, Doc. Fit as a flea.'

Sally straightened. He had said his daughter had got divorced, and from his tone of voice he had found it very stressful. Stress was a typical trigger for herpes zoster, and in the absence of any other symptoms it was her most likely diagnosis, even without the rash.

'I'm not sure,' she told him,' 'but I think you might be getting shingles. You've got the classic symptoms. If I'm right, you should get a rash soon over the sore bit, small raised red spots that turn into chicken-pox-type blisters and then scab over. Now, I'm going to give you a presciption for an antiviral drug that should limit the severity of the disease, but there's nothing I can do to stop it. If it is herpes zoster or shingles, you'll find it will last about two to three weeks, and then you should be feeling much better.'

'And if it isn't?'

'It could be pleurisy, but you haven't got the classic pain radiating up to your shoulder when you breathe in and, frankly, I think it's highly unlikely. Have you ever had chicken-pox?'

He nodded. 'I believe so, as a child. I seem to

remember my mother putting cotton gloves on me and smothering me in calamine lotion.'

Sally smiled. 'Sounds like it, then. Right, here's your prescription. Follow the instructions, and let me know if there's any change. If you deteriorate, or if the rash doesn't come out and the pain gets worse, give me a ring.'

As he stood to put on his shirt, Sally noticed a slightly reddened area under his arm.

'Hang on,' she said, and, lifting his arm again, she inspected the skin more closely. Sure enough, a very fine scatter of pink pinpricks was beginning to spread over a tiny area high up on his ribs near his armpit.

'Yes, I can see the rash now, only very faintly but it's starting. Right, get those antiviral pills started as soon as possible, and hopefully your symptoms won't be too bad and they will limit the severity of the pain. You can take simple painkillers, like paracetamol, but if it's too bad come back to me and I'll give you something stronger. Hopefully we won't need to do that.'

Sally glanced at her watch as he left. Six-fifteen. With any luck her last couple of patients wouldn't take too long, and then she could escape. She was starving, and it seemed ages since that half-bowl of soup at lunchtime.

Her next patient, however, snookered her hopes of a quick escape.

Carol Bailey had the butterfly of an ear-ring embedded in the back of her ear-lobe, and the lobe had swollen and become extremely inflamed and infected.

'Oh, dear,' Sally said sympathetically. 'That must be very sore.'

The girl nodded. 'It is. I thought it was getting a bit

tender, so I put a plaster on it. Didn't think to take the ear-ring out, because I've worn them for years and quite often they get a bit sore. I had some cheap earrings on this time, and that's when it happens. Anyway, I went to take it out and the back seemed to have disappeared. Then my mum said it was stuck in the back of my ear.'

'Yes, it is. I'll have to give you a local anaesthetic and make a tiny cut just to pop that out. Are you allergic to any local anaesthetics, do you know? Do you have an injection at the dentist?'

She nodded. 'Yeah. No problems.'

'Good. I'll give you the injection, then I'm going to ask you to go and wait in the waiting-room while I see my next patient. That'll give the anaesthetic time to work.'

She drew up a small amount of lignocaine, and injected the ear-lobe with it.

'Ouch!' Carol exclaimed.

'Sorry. It can be a bit sore going in. Right, if you could send in the last patient for me——'

'The last? There's about four out there.'

'Oh. Right. Well, the next, then. Thanks.'

She rang Jackie. 'Have I got extra patients?'

'Yes—sorry, I was about to ring you. There are two of them. They've got their notes with them.'

Sally sighed under her breath, smiled at the next patient and carried on.

Fortunately they were all simple cases: tonsillitis, an abscess that would need excision in the morning, and a urinary infection. She dealt with them all accordingly, called the girl with the ear-ring back in and quickly excised the butterfly clip.

'Can I have it back?' Carol asked. 'Only the ear-rings are useless without it.'

'I should chuck them out, if I were you,' Sally advised. 'The butterfly's very small and could easily get stuck again. I should let this heal for at least a week before you try and put another ear-ring in.'

'But it'll heal!'

Sally hung on to her temper with difficulty. 'That's rather the idea.'

'But I don't want the hole to heal up. Here, I've brought a gold ring with me—could you put that in? It'll keep the hole open and the rest can heal. It's happened before.'

Sally looked at her ears, festooned with several studs. She didn't doubt she'd had problems.

'I'm sorry,' she said firmly. 'There's no way I'm putting anything in that ear, and if you do I can't be held responsible for the consequences. You've got a very nasty infection, and you really ought to take it seriously. I'm giving you some antibiotics to take, and I want you to be sure and take them so that infection doesn't spread.'

'Antibiotics?' Carol asked, clearly amazed.

'Antibiotics,' Sally repeated firmly.

The girl reluctantly took her prescription and left, and Sally stood up and scooped up the notes, took her handbag out of the drawer and headed towards the office.

Jackie greeted her with a little sheaf of messages.

'Three calls—two in town, quite close, and one out in a village on your way home.'

'Wonderful. Just what I needed. How urgent are they?'

Jackie shrugged. 'Depends if you're the doctor or

the patient, I guess. Nothing critical, I don't think. I'm going home to my husband and children.'

Sally smiled at her wearily. 'You do that. I'll see you tomorrow. Thanks.'

She did the calls on the way home, if only to get them out of the way before the rest started. As Jackie had said, they weren't critical. Two of the people could easily have made it to the surgery earlier, and the third could have waited till the morning. Still, at least they wouldn't get her out in the middle of the night. . .

It was nearly nine before she got home, and Sam was dozing in the middle of the settee in the sitting-room when she got back, a sleeping child under each arm.

They looked gorgeous: Molly with her dark hair straggling across one cheek, her lashes black against her pale skin; Ben, his face thinner now as he began to mature, a carbon copy of his father; and Sam, long legs stretched out, his dark gold hair tousled, his mouth soft and full and very kissable.

She blinked. Kissable? That was an unfamiliar urge. It had been ages since she'd wanted to kiss him, really kiss him till she blew his socks off.

And now was hardly the time.

'It's lovely to see you all so busy,' she said softly.

One by one their eyes opened and they struggled to wakefulness.

'Hello, Mum,' Ben mumbled.

'We waited up for you,' Molly said sleepily.

She met Sam's heavy-lidded eyes, and he quirked his brows. 'I didn't think you'd be this late.' His voice was husky with sleep, and it made her tingle.

'I had three calls after surgery, and it was one of those long evenings. Is there anything to eat? I'm starving.'

'Yes, in the oven. Let me get the kids into bed and I'll join you. Come on, kids, up the wooden hill to Bedfordshire.'

She kissed the children, then watched as he scooped the sleepy Molly into his arms and followed Ben slowly up the stairs. He looked stiff, from sitting still for so long, presumably.

Bless them. Fancy waiting up for her. Her eyes prickled with tears and she dashed them impatiently away and kicked off her shoes, sinking down on to the settee in Sam's place.

It was warm from his body, soothing, and she reached out for a cushion and tucked it under her cheek, snuggling into the back of the settee. She didn't sleep, just lay there in his warmth and tried to relax.

No wonder he so often came home for lunch and dropped off to sleep. Napping was very healthy, she knew, but it was something she'd never learned to do.

Perhaps she just needed more practice!

She heard Sam's footsteps, and lifted her head half an inch to smile wearily at him.

'Hi.'

He sat down awkwardly beside her.

'Hi.'

She peered at him. 'You look stiff—what have you been doing?'

'Oh, don't. I went to your health club and chatted up one of the fitness instructors to let me use your membership for the next couple of weeks.'

'And?'

'She let me make a fool of myself.'

Sally tried to hide the smile. 'But I thought you'd find it dead easy, playing about at the health club? After all, I do it——'

'Don't, Sally,' he warned.

'What's the matter, baby? Your ego dented?'

'Witch,' he mumbled, and shifted painfully. 'God, my legs hurt. That treadmill's a killer.'

'It gets easier,' she promised.

He muttered something unprintable, and she chuckled.

'Don't wind me up or I won't feed you,' he warned. Her stomach grumbled, and Sam got painfully to his feet.

'Come on, then,' he said, and she could have sworn he was glad to get away from her—or the conversation? She wondered what had happened.

'Who was the instructor?' she asked idly, following him into the kitchen.

'What? Oh, Amy.'

Sally nodded. Amy would be sensible, but she wasn't above letting him make a fool of himself for fun. She turned away so Sam wouldn't see the smile.

At three in the morning the phone rang, and she stumbled out of bed, threw on her clothes and told Sam to ring an ambulance and send it to Sue Palmer's house.

She arrived there before the ambulance, but fortunately it wasn't far behind her because Sue was pale, clammy and in a lot of pain. She had also noticed a small vaginal blood loss, and Sally was very worried that the placenta had separated from the uterus and that she was haemorrhaging. Often the mother's condition was out of all proportion to the apparent loss, and Sue certainly looked as if she'd lost more than the small amount she reported.

While she waited for the ambulance Sally got an

intravenous line in and began running in saline and 10 mg of cyclimorph for the pain.

The ambulance arrived just as she completed the injection, and she handed a hastily scribbled letter to them and rang the maternity unit on her mobile phone after the ambulance had left.

Please, God, she thought, let the baby be all right. Don't let me have killed it because I didn't act soon enough.

Shocked, worried, her professional confidence in tatters, she drove home to find Sam in the kitchen boiling the kettle.

'How is she?'

'Weak, shocked—oh, Sam, what if the baby dies?'

He squeezed her shoulder, well aware of what she was going through.

'Don't jump the gun,' he advised gently. 'Here, I've made tea. Let's go in the sitting-room.'

She trailed after him. 'Should I have admitted her earlier?'

'I don't know. I didn't see her. Did you go back?'

'Yes. Yes, I did, and she was no different—tired, perhaps, but nothing untoward.'

'Then, no, I don't think you could have been expected to admit her earlier. What for, as you said?'

Sally sighed heavily and curled her feet under her bottom. 'A gut instinct?'

He shrugged. 'Looks odd on paper. How was her husband?'

'Calm, organised—marvellous, really. Very supportive, but worried to death.'

Sam pushed a mug into her hand and made her drink some tea. It lay heavily in her stomach, though, so she just cradled the cup for comfort.

'Any more calls?' she asked belatedly.

'No. How's it been going?'

She gave a hollow laugh. 'Fine till now. Sam, what if the baby dies?'

'Did you get a heartbeat at the house?'

'I didn't try—there wasn't time, and I didn't want to muck about.'

'Ring the hospital.'

'Should I?'

'Of course. I would.'

She picked up the phone and dialled the hospital, and after a moment she was transferred to the theatre.

'She went into surgery with a strong heartbeat from the baby, so hopefully—hang on, can you? I'll go and ask.'

Sally heard footsteps walking away from the phone, murmured words in the background and then footsteps approaching again.

Her palms were clammy, her heart pounding.

'Hello? The baby's fine. The placenta was still partly attached. OK?'

'Thank you,' Sally said, and put the phone down with trembling fingers.

'Sally?'

'The baby's fine,' she said unsteadily, and turning, she threw herself into Sam's waiting arms.

CHAPTER FOUR

Poor Sally. She'd had a tough night, worrying about Sue Palmer and her baby. Still, medicine was like that, totally unpredictable.

Personally he would have admitted her earlier, Sam thought, but it was hard to say. Judging by Sally's account, there had been little to go on.

Still, no harm done. They probably wouldn't have done much in hospital for the first twenty-four hours. A scan, perhaps, but that wasn't always conclusive.

It was a beautiful morning. He dropped the children off at school and went to the health club, where Amy put him through a nice, steady routine that nevertheless made his aching muscles howl in protest.

When he got back he was greeted by a mountainous washing-basket in the utility-room. Unready to tackle it, he made a cup of coffee and took it out into the garden, walking round and studying the beds.

Sally was right; she had done a lot of work out here.

The front, though, needed some attention. He had noticed large areas which were infested with weeds, all at the seedling stage. If he hoed them out now for her, she wouldn't have nearly so much to do later.

And then, after lunch, he'd tackle the washing.

Sue Palmer's haemorrhage was a frightening lesson in the sharp end of medicine for Sally. Sam had been wonderful, kind and supportive, without a word of criticism or censure, not a trace of an 'I told you so', and yet she was sure he would have admitted the woman sooner.

Intuition, or experience? Experience, she was sure, because *she* had known something was badly wrong, so why hadn't she acted more quickly?

Because she had no proof, and she didn't want to appear trigger-happy.

Well, to hell with how she looked. From now on, if she had the slightest doubt, she would admit willy-nilly and regardless. Let the hospital make the tricky decisions and send patients home unfit.

She had rung the hospital again in the morning for an update, and was delighted to hear that both mother and baby—a girl—were doing well.

It was a good job someone was, she thought, because lack of sleep meant she was doing decidedly indifferently. She struggled against weariness all morning, and when lunchtime came she headed for home, hoping for a lazy hour curled up on the settee in the sitting-room before her antenatal clinic at three.

Her tiredness was banished, however, when she turned into the drive to see Sam hard at work in the front garden with a hoe.

For all his other qualities, Sam was not a gardener—and he was hoeing right in the middle of her pansies!

She leapt out of the car and rushed over to where he was putting the finishing touches to the carnage.

'Hi!' he said cheerfully. 'Looks better, doesn't it?'

Her shoulders drooped. 'Oh, Sam,' she wailed 'you've hoed up all my pansy seedlings!'

Lunch was conducted in a huffy silence, with Sam defensive and Sally tired, crabby and unreasonable.

'Why didn't you ask?' she had yelled at him.

'Ask what? They looked like weeds! What was I

suppose to say? "Sally, can I dig this weed up?" Life's too short.'

'Clearly—for the pansies.'

'Oh, stuff the bloody pansies,' he had yelled, and stalked off into the house in a rage.

Now, after lunch, things weren't a great deal better.

'Just promise me something,' she begged. 'Don't do anything else in the garden without asking me first, eh?'

'Does that apply to my patients, as well?'

She sighed. 'Sam, it's hardly the same. At least I'm trained.'

'Is that why you didn't admit Sue Palmer until it was almost too late?' he said softly.

The words hung in the air between them, vibrating in the silence.

Shocked, as much by the truth of his remark as by the pain of his criticism, Sally could scarcely drag the air into her lungs.

'That was uncalled-for,' she managed finally, her voice uneven.

He stabbed his hands though his hair and let his breath out in a gush. 'Hell, I'm sorry. I don't know why I said it.'

Sally swallowed hard. 'Because it's true?' she whispered.

He sighed and closed his eyes. He couldn't deny it, they both knew that. 'You did what you thought was right at the time,' he said eventually.

'I was wrong.'

'Not necessarily.'

'Stop trying to make it better, Sam. I was wrong. You know it and I know it. Sue Palmer knows it. I expect the GMC will know it before long.'

He swivelled towards her. 'She's not taking action against you?'

Sally shook her head. 'Not as far as I'm aware.'

His shoulders dropped a fraction in relief. 'God, for a moment there I thought. . .'

He stood up and went into the kitchen, switching on the kettle. 'Have a cup of tea before you go back.'

'No.' She followed him out. 'I won't. I want to get back to those antenatal notes and study them line by line before those women come in. If any of them has so much as a head cold, she'll be admitted.'

She tugged on her coat, picked up her bag and keys and was just going out of the door when Sam's voice stopped her.

'Sally?'

She turned. 'Yes?'

'I'm sorry.'

She swallowed hard. 'It's OK.'

'No—no, it's not. It was unfair. You did what you thought was right on the evidence you had. It's all very well having twenty-twenty hindsight, but it could have been wind.'

Sally smiled wearily. 'Thanks, Sam—not for the lies, but for bothering to tell them.'

'They aren't——'

'Save it. And stay out of my garden. If you've got time on your hands, you could tackle the washing. I'm nearly out of knickers.'

'I'd better do it then, hadn't I? Can't have my wife running around with that sassy little backside all naked.'

She laughed. 'Sam, it's years since I had a sassy little backside.'

His eyes glittered. 'Don't you believe it,' he said softly.

She bolted.

True to her word, Sally checked and rechecked every set of notes before the first antenatal patient crossed her threshold that afternoon.

Perhaps because of her vigilance, she thought she detected an abnormal heartbeat in one baby. She asked the midwife running the clinic with her to check, and she agreed. The heartbeat was irregular, sometimes gappy, and Sally was concerned.

'Is there something wrong?' the woman asked.

'Probably not,' Sally hastened to assure her. 'The baby's heartbeat is a little irregular, that's all. Usually it doesn't mean anything, but I think to be on the safe side you ought to let them check you out at the hospital.'

The baby was nearly term and, checking the co-op card, she discovered that the woman hadn't been scanned yet.

'They'll probaby want you to have a scan, to have a look at the baby's heart,' Sally said. 'I'll send you with a letter. If you ask at reception they'll ring and get an appointment through for you in the next day or so, but please don't worry. It's probably absolutely nothing, but I'd hate to neglect it.'

While the woman was in transit from the consulting-room to the reception office, Sally rang through.

'Mavis, get Mrs Clarke an appointment for a scan as quick as possible, please. There's an abnormal heartbeat and I want it checked out fast, but don't worry her.'

'Right, I'll do that in my room,' Mavis promised,

and Sally left her to it and went back to her other patients.

Fortunately they were all doing well, with no nasty abnormalities or hiccups, and when the clinic was over Sally went into the kitchen and made herself a cup of tea.

Mavis found her there. 'She's gone straight down. I told her they'd got a cancellation, but her consultant was running a clinic this afternoon and he said he wanted to see her at once, so he was fitting her in.'

'Excellent.'

'Oh, and Mr Palmer rang, to say his wife and the baby are fine and thank you for all your help yesterday and in the night. He was really grateful because you were so prompt.'

Sally, who had her own very clear feelings on the matter, said nothing.

Sam opened the door of the washing-machine and stared in horrified disbelief.

Pink!

Everything was pink—his shirts, Sally's underwear, Molly's school socks and blouse, the white checks in Ben's school shirt—everything.

Sally would go ape.

Wondering bleakly how else he could foul up today, he pulled the soggy pink mess out into the plastic basket and studied it dismally, sifting through the contents in increasing despair.

Six of his shirts—six, for heaven's sake! And loads of knickers—his, Sally's, Molly's—oh, lord, and Ben's. Ben would take *really* well to having pink knickers!

Maybe it would wash out.

He turned the dial to a hot wash, stuffed all the

things back in, bar the offending red T-shirt, and switched the machine on again.

An hour later, he had achieved nothing—well, nothing positive.

His white polycotton work shirts were now perma-creased as well as pink, and the elastic in all the knickers had collapsed.

Defeated, he threw the whole mess into the tumble-drier and switched it on.

Sally had said it wasn't working properly, but he couldn't see anything wrong with it. The clothes went round and round, and the air was coming out warm.

He went into the kitchen and turned his attention to supper. This, he thought, couldn't fail.

A range of cold meats, salad and boiled new potatoes.

All he had to do was not overcook the potatoes, and it would be fine.

It was late—again—by the time Sally's surgery finished. She went home armed with the knowledge that Jo Clarke's baby had an irregular heart trace confirmed by the hospital, who had phoned to warn her that they were inducing her the following morning and she might very well be in touch.

Sally could hardly wait. Interviews like that were always difficult, because there was nothing to add until the baby was born and could be examined after the changes in circulation that happened at birth had taken place. Until then it was all a case of speculation, and she really didn't feel she could cope. She would talk to Sam and ask him to deal with it, as he was the Clarkes' proper GP and she felt he ought to be the person to discuss such news with them.

After all, there was no reason why he couldn't, just because she was covering the majority of his work.

A little bit of her was conscious of ducking out of a painful chore, but she justified it on the grounds of the well-being of the patient being better served if it was Sam who dealt with it.

Anyway, she'd have to talk to him first.

She turned into the drive and stared, amazed.

A thin plume of smoke was filtering up behind the house. Was Sam having a bonfire?

Now? At seven o'clock?

Anything was possible.

It didn't smell like a bonfire, though.

She opened the garage door and was immediately assailed by the acrid smell of smoke.

The house!

She flung open the door into the utility-room and was greeted by the sight of flames inside the tumble-drier.

'Sam!' she screamed, and he came running into the kitchen.

'What is it, for God's sake?'

'The tumble-drier!' she said, pointing, and, without hesitating, he yanked the plug out, pulled the hose off the back and picked the flaming machine up in his arms.

'Open the door,' he snapped, and she flung the door wide and watched in amazement as he carried the machine out into the garden and dumped it unceremoniously on the ground.

Opening the door of the machine, he hurled a bucket of water into the flaming core and stood back to watch as the flames died instantly and stinking, acrid steam belched out into the cool night air.

'Hell's teeth, that was a close one,' he said. 'Good job you got back when you did.'

Sally was speechless.

'You knew it wasn't working properly,' she squeaked, finding her voice at last. 'I told you it had started overheating—that was why I hadn't been using it.'

He shot her a fulminating glance. 'I didn't realise it was that sort of not working,' he muttered tersely. 'Ouch, my arms hurt.'

Sally looked down at his bare forearms. Already they were reddening and looked sore.

She took his watch off. 'You need cold water on them straight away,' she told him and, leading him back into the kitchen, she ran a deep bowl of cold water and instructed him to plunge both forearms in up to the elbow.

'Not exactly comfortable,' he said drily, leaning his elbows on the bottom of the sink and watching her as she took some sterile dressing out of the first-aid cupboard.

'Tough. At least you'll sleep. Here, sit on this.'

There was an old stool she used for sitting at the sink preparing vegetables, and she pushed it up behind him so he could perch on it.

'A sensible person, of course,' she said mildly, watching as he wafted his sore arms through the water, 'would have pulled the plug out and used the fire-extinguisher on the wall beside it.'

'Now she tells me,' he groaned.

'I expect you just wanted to impress me with your heroics.'

He snorted rudely. 'Fat lot of good it did.'

She chuckled. 'What was in there?' she asked out of interest.

He went a fascinating shade of brick-red on the back of his neck.

'Sam?' she prodded.

'All sorts of things—your undies, Molly's socks, Ben's school shirt, all my white shirts—whites, really.'

Sally was confused. 'Whites? But everything looked pink——'

'It's the light,' he said, but too quickly.

'It is?'

She went out into the garden and came back in with the soggy, charred remains of a pink shirt.

'Funny light—seems to be the same in here, too.'

'So I had an accident.'

She buried the smile. 'I gather.'

He sighed. 'You might as well know the rest. I tried to get the colour out by boil-washing everything.'

'Boil. . . But your shirts are all polycotton! And the knicker-elastic——'

'All right, so it was a mistake!'

She couldn't hide the smile any longer. 'So you decided to set fire to everything. I don't know, the lengths some people will go to to destroy the evidence!'

A soggy dish-cloth hit her squarely in the face.

Peeling it off, she threw it back and then regarded him thoughtfully. 'So, do I have any clean knickers for the morning?'

'No—and Molly hasn't got any other socks to wear, and my shirts are all wrecked.'

She heaved a sigh. 'OK. You'd better go to Marks and Spencer in the morning and replace everything.'

'It'll cost a fortune,' he grumbled.

'Mmm. Even more than fixing your car—and then

there's the cost of the tumble-drier to take into consideration. Is there any supper?'

'Yes. Do you suppose we could claim on the insurance?'

'Even though I'd told you it wasn't cutting out and was overheating? I think not. I'll go and change into my night things, then I'll put in a load of washing so we've got something to wear tomorrow—and if you know what's good for you, you'll stay out of the utility-room!'

'My pleasure,' he muttered.

'Tut, tut—don't be ungracious!'

He swore softly.

'Sam!'

She couldn't resist swatting him on the bottom as she passed.

Sam glared balefully at his sore, reddened arms.

Such gratitude, he thought miserably. Trust Sally to think of the fire-extinguisher *after* he'd burned himself.

He eased his arms out of the icy water and inspected them curiously. Only slight burns, except for that small area that was blistering on his right wrist. He'd put a clean dressing on that bit, but the rest would have to lump it. He couldn't spend the entire night immersed in the sink listening to Sally teasing him.

He carefully patted his arms dry and reflected on what a bloody awful day it had been. First the pansies, then the row about Sue Palmer's baby—he could still kick himself for that—then the washing, and now his arms were sore and Sally had scored another round.

Damn.

As days went, it really had been the pits.

Still, tomorrow would be different. He would go out

first thing and replace all their clothes, and he'd get a new tumble-drier to replace the one he'd cremated, and while he was at it he'd buy a Teasmade so he didn't have to get up at that ungodly hour to give Sally her morning fix of tea.

Good idea.

And perhaps tomorrow he'd manage an edible meal. Of course, he still had Sally's comments on the bullet-hard new potatoes to deal with. He didn't doubt they would be forthcoming.

Still, at least she was teasing him now, not just turning away in grim-lipped silence. It dawned on him just how long it had been since she'd teased him.

Years.

Maybe it was progress of a sort.

Funny progress, having to turn yourself into a figure of fun to get your wife to laugh again—and then at you instead of with you.

Great.

His arms hurt. Morosely, wallowing in self-pity and disgust, he took the salad out of the fridge and put in on the table. Oh, well, it looked pretty enough.

After all, no-one was perfect. . .

Jo Clarke's baby was born the following afternoon, and the ECG showed no abnormality. Sally's relief was enormous. The last thing she'd needed was another crisis.

She had phoned the hospital just before her evening surgery and been given the news, and had rung Sam straight away.

'I said you were over-reacting,' he told her calmly.

'Have you been shopping to replace my clothes?' she asked waspishly.

'Of course—and the supper's in the oven. I'm just taking the kids to Cubs and Brownies, and I'll be back later with them. Julia's car's broken down so I said I'd take her brood as well.'

'How noble,' Sally commented. 'What's for supper?'

'Roast chicken.'

Sally's stomach rumbled. She had been too busy for lunch, and by the time she'd finished here she would be ready to chew the legs off the kitchen table. She said goodbye to Sam and threw herself into her evening surgery with renewed enthusiasm.

Sam couldn't believe it. The chicken should have been nicely browned, the roast potatoes crisp and golden, and instead there was the same pallid, cold, unappetising blob surrounded by raw grey potatoes.

He glowered at the oven controls. He had set them to come on, for heaven's sake! The timer looked as it ought to, so why. . .?

The oven temperature. He hadn't set the oven temperature, and the potatoes were now ruined.

Disgusted with his inept stupidity, he nearly wrenched the switch off the front of the cooker.

It started to hum most gratifyingly—about two hours too late.

Damn.

He threw the potatoes in the bin, peeled the last few and put them in.

'We need a bath,' the children told him.

'No time.'

'But we can do it ourselves,' Ben assured him.

He glanced distractedly at his son. 'Sure?'

'Yes, of course.' Such scorn.

'OK, but don't make a mess.'

They disappeared like greased lightning, leaving Sam struggling with the vegetables and a sinking feeling in the pit of his stomach.

That chicken wasn't going to be ready till nearly nine o'clock.

He closed his eyes in despair and nearly took the end off his thumb.

Sally walked in on a scene of chaos. A trail of blood ran across the floor into the utility-room, and she followed it to find Sam struggling one-handed with the plasters.

'What on earth have you done?' she asked in concern.

He stuck his thumb out to show her, and fresh blood welled out of the cut.

'Ouch.'

'Hmm. Can you stick something on it?'

'Sure.' She dried it carefully, then put a plaster on, tugging the edges together. It looked a nasty cut, deep and very sore. 'You'd better keep that dry,' she advised him.

'Does that mean you'll do the vegetables?' he asked hopefully.

She laughed, fighting her instincts. 'No chance, mate—wear gloves. You'll have to do a lot better than that to get yourself invalided out. When's supper?'

'Ah.'

'Ah?'

'The oven timer didn't work.'

'It didn't?'

Sam gritted his teeth. 'I forgot to turn on the oven temperature.'

She made a small round O with her lips and turned silently on her heel. 'Fine. Have the children eaten?'

'They had sweets—they're in the bath now.'

'Sweets won't keep them going——'

'They had a king-sized Mars bar each.'

'What!'

'It's the first time——'

'And the last. I bet they didn't tell you they aren't allowed king-sized Mars bars because they can't eat their supper afterwards?'

'No, they didn't,' he snapped, 'but as I've fouled up in that department again, perhaps it's just as well they're not hungry!'

He stomped over to the sink, and Sally had to hold herself down to stop herself from hugging him.

No, she didn't! What was she thinking about?

She went up behind him and slid her arms round his waist.

He stiffened instantly and turned in her arms, his hands held out to the side. Reaching up on tiptoe, she kissed him gently on the lips.

'What's that for?' he asked suspiciously.

'Because you look as if you've had a lousy day— because I'm sorry you've cut your thumb—because. . .' She hesitated. Because what? Because she loved him? The realisation struck her with all the force of a truck. She mustn't tell him, though—not yet, so soon. There was too much still to be done, too much ground to cover before their relationship was truly stable and back on track again. She reached up and brushed his hair off his forehead, so that she could touch him. 'Just because,' she finished huskily.

His eyes searched hers, and she saw desire flicker to life in their ice-blue depths.

'Sally,' he groaned, and his head lowered towards her.

He's going to kiss me, she thought, and a shiver of desire rippled through her.

A scream cut through the air, and she shot backwards out of his arms.

'What was that?'

'Molly,' he said with a groan.

'Oh, God.'

She ran trembling hands through her hair, then turned on her heel and headed for the stairs.

'I should put the chicken in the microwave for about ten minutes to speed it up,' she yelled over her shoulder, then took the stairs two at a time to sort out the chaos in the bathroom.

CHAPTER FIVE

SALLY was on duty on Saturday morning till midday, covering an emergency surgery and a few visits. One of the calls she had to make was to David Jones, the man with shingles.

'I can't believe how painful it is,' he told her miserably. 'I can't sleep, I can't find a comfortable position, and every time I doze off I turn over and wake myself up.'

Sally turned back the bedclothes and inspected the rash. It was extremely angry and the spots had turned yellow and were beginning to crust over. Once they had dried, the crusts would fall off and the worst would be over—provided he didn't then suffer from post-herpetic neuralgia, a distressingly painful condition that was notoriously difficult to treat.

Hopefully the prompt use of antiviral drugs would have an effect on the severity of that particularly nasty complication.

In the meantime, though, he needed painkillers, strong ones that would really work.

She wrote him up for a paracetamol and dihydrocodeine preparation that was usually sufficiently powerful to block most pain, and also warned him about the danger of constipation with the codeine.

'That's the least of my worries,' he said unhappily, and Sally gave him a couple of the tablets to start him off until his wife was able to get the prescription at the chemist.

She had another call to make that morning, to Mr Lucas, the first patient she had seen at the beginning of the week who had got her return to work off to such a flying start with his grumbling sarcasm and thinly-veiled criticism of working women.

His bronchitis was playing up again, his wife said, and he could hardly breathe.

She found him in a very poor condition, and her instincts were immediately aroused. He looked awful, blue around the mouth, his eyes slightly glazed.

She took his pulse, listened to his chest, then sat back on her heels beside his chair and took his hand.

'Mr Lucas, I want you to go into hospital. Your chest is in a very bad way, and I think you need oxygen and I'd like a consultant to see you. Is that all right?'

He shot her a dirty look. Nothing wrong with his temper, she thought drily.

'I think it's important to get you the right care, Mr Lucas.'

'Your husband wouldn't send me in,' he told her bluntly. 'Just because you don't feel competent to deal with me at home——'

'Are you refusing to be admitted, Mr Lucas?' she asked him tersely.

'Oh, Fred, please do go,' his wife begged. 'You had such a bad night, love—I really think she's right——'

'Mind your own business, woman!' he muttered, then bent over, racked with a savage cough.

Mrs Lucas stood beside Sally, wringing her hands together in despair. 'Oh, he must go in—he must!'

'I'll ring my husband. Perhaps he can convince him,' Sally muttered. 'May I use your phone?'

'Of course, dear.'

She explained the situation to Sam in a few carefully chosen words, and he snorted. 'I'll be right over.'

He arrived a few minutes later, took one look at Lucas and shook his head.

'Good lord, man, what are you thinking about? You should be in hospital already—probably days ago!'

'She didn't say anything about that on Monday,' he croaked.

'She' clamped her teeth shut and said nothing.

'You saw him?' Sam asked.

'Yes. His chest was fairly clear, but he was complaining of breathlessness. I put him on antibiotics, told him to give up smoking, and wrote to the hospital asking for an appointment with a chest physician. I also,' she added, glaring at Mr Lucas, 'told him to tell me if it got any worse.'

'I was just as bad then.'

'Not like this. Mr Lucas, if you'd been like this you couldn't have got to the surgery.'

'That's true, Fred—you were nothing like this bad on Monday. Don't tell lies to get Mrs Alexander into trouble, it isn't fair.'

He harumphed and folded his arms across his thin, weedy chest, and Sam winked at Sally.

'Right, you'd better call an ambulance and arrange his admission,' he told her.

'He hasn't yet agreed to go,' Sally reminded him.

'Nonsense. You'll go, won't you, Fred?'

'Might. Then again I might not.'

Sally quirked an eyebrow at Sam, but he just grinned.

'Call them. He'll go, if I have to knock him out.'

They waited together until the ambulance arrived to

take him away, then stood on the kerb outside the house watching it retreat.

'Looks nasty—more than just pneumonia.'

'CA lung on top?' Sally asked.

'Very likely. He's refused all tests and X-rays in the past, but this time I think he's really scared.'

'Hmm. Well, if it is lung cancer, he's got something to be scared about now.'

'Absolutely. I'd give him less than a week, frankly.'

She smiled up at him wearily. 'You wouldn't like to make that three weeks, would you, so you can deal with Mrs Lucas?'

'I'll deal with her anyway,' he promised.

She was relieved. Terminal care of long-time patients wasn't a job for the locum.

Her stomach, no respecter of persons or events, rumbled.

'Hungry?'

'Mmm. Have you cooked anything?'

'No. How about a pub lunch?'

'What about the children? Where are they? I thought you'd brought them.'

He shook his head. 'I dropped them off at my parents' this morning—Mum was taking them to the cinema.'

'So we're alone?'

'Uh-huh. So, pub?'

She grinned. 'What a good idea.'

'The Dirty Duck?'

'I'll follow you.'

They swapped a smile, then Sally ran to the little Peugeot, started the engine and followed the Mercedes to the pub by the river where they had often gone before the children came along.

'It hasn't changed at all,' Sally said wistfully, glancing round at the heavy beams gleaming with horse-brasses, the magnificent inglenook fireplace where they had often sat warming themselves in that first winter of their courtship. Not that they had needed much warming. . .

Her first day in general practice had been awful—busy, riddled with enigmas, peppered with the sort of trivia she had never met in hospital medicine. She had been terrified of doing the wrong thing, filling in the wrong form or just plain missing something vital in a sea of malingerers and hypochondriacs.

She finished her evening surgery after everyone else, of course, even though she only had a handful of patients.

She emerged from her surgery cautiously, half expecting to be mugged by half a dozen angry patients who had been filed in the wrong room and were furious about being kept waiting.

Instead she found Sam, slouched comfortably at the scruffy old table in the practice kitchen, a cup of tea in one hand and a paper in the other.

He looked up and grinned. 'All done?'

'At last,' she said wearily and sank down on another chair, kicking her shoes off and wriggling her toes in relief. 'What a lot of fuss-pots.'

He laughed. 'They just want to meet the new doctor. There probably wasn't a genuine complaint among them.'

He folded the paper and set it down on the table, then stretched his arms up above his head with a satisfied groan.

'All finished till tomorrow.'

She gave a weak smile. 'I'm sure it will be just as endless as today.'

He chuckled. 'You'll soon get used to it. You'll learn to work faster, and it'll all fall into place in no time.'

He glanced at his watch. 'Are you doing anything tonight?'

'Dying,' she said theatrically.

'Anything else? Anything more pressing?'

She laughed, unable to resist his twinkling blue eyes and sexy grin.

'Nothing more pressing, no.'

'How about grabbing a bite in a pub I know? The food's cheap, nourishing and plentiful, the atmosphere's thick with history and the landlord's a patient.'

She frowned curiously. 'What does that mean?'

'It means he treats me like royalty because he's worried he might need me one day!'

Sally laughed again. 'Ok. Do I need to change?'

'No, you're fine, unless you'd rather?'

She shook her head. 'I'm starving.'

'Me too. Come on. Is your car here?'

She shook her head again. 'No, my flat's only round the corner so I walked.'

'We'll take mine, then.'

He ushered her out of the door, locking up and setting the alarm as he went, and then helped her into the car.

He had manners, she had to give him that. There was no question of leaving her to fend for herself.

She watched, fascinated, as he slid behind the wheel and started the engine, then pulled smoothly out of the car park.

He had very sexy wrists, she mused, lightly dusted with gold hairs to match the soft, thick mane on his head. His hands were strong, she noted. Strong and straight, the fingers long and blunt, square-tipped and confident on the controls.

She wondered how his hands would feel on her body, and was shocked at herself.

Heavens, she'd only met him briefly during the day—once before at her interview, but that was hardly protracted.

Still, she could hardly take her eyes off those hands, and when they turned into the pub she had to force herself to look quickly away before he caught her staring.

The pub supper was excellent—a rump steak in a squashy bap with salad on the side, and apple pie and cream to follow.

She ate every scrap, to Sam's approval, and then they sat and talked for hours.

He was witty, charming, fun to be with and yet serious when the conversation got round to medicine as it inevitably did.

She discovered that he was deeply compassionate, committed to preventive medicine and very much against the willy-nilly prescribing of antibiotics.

'There are so many things now that are resistant to antibiotics just because of over-use,' he told her. 'Often all patients need is reassurance that they will get better and nothing awful is wrong, then they can go home and get on with the business of being ill in peace. It's all quite natural, and did we but remember it, our bodies are well-equipped to deal with it.'

'It's all so different from hospital medicine.'

'It needs to be—the patients aren't that ill, or they wouldn't be in our care.' He tapped her glass. 'Another one?'

'I'd better not, I have to concentrate tomorrow and having a hangover won't help me at all,' she said with a smile.

'You'll cope,' he told her confidently.

They went out into the cold, bright night, and he drove back towards the town, parking outside her flat in the quiet side street.

She didn't want the evening to end. It had been such good fun, and she had really enjoyed his company. She turned towards him in the car.

'Would you like a cup of coffee? It's only instant with powdered creamer, but you're welcome if you want.'

He grinned. 'It's all I have at home. Housekeeping isn't one of my skills.'

She laughed. 'Nor mine. Oh, well, I'll have to find a wife to look after me.'

'I hope you have better luck than me. I'd love a wife to look after me, but I've never found anyone I'd like to spend my life with, and I'd rather do my own cooking, lousy though I am, than compromise on something so important.'

She met his eyes, surprised and pleased by his genuine response to her flippant remark.

'Me, too,' she said softly.

Their eyes held for an age, then Sam drew in a slow breath and opened the car door. 'Coffee?'

'Good idea.'

She let them into her flat and put the kettle on before heading into her bedroom and kicking off her shoes. She felt uncomfortable in her clothes, too formal for slouching about.

'Put the fire on, I'll be with you in a tick,' she called,

and, pulling off her clothes, she dived quickly into jeans and a sloppy sweater and her scruffy old slippers.

That was better. Tugging out her ponytail, she shook her hair loose and brushed it quickly, then went back into the little living-room.

Sam was sitting on the floor by the fire, flicking through a home interiors magazine.

'Bit of a contrast,' he said, his grin wry as he glanced round the room.

She chuckled. 'Dismal, isn't it? Still, it's only for a year, then hopefully I'll get a real job somewhere and put down some roots.'

'You might end up staying on here,' he said. 'I did. Martin Goody's senior partner trained me, and when he retired at the end of my year Martin became the senior partner and took me on.'

'Are you happy here?'

'Oh, yes. Martin's great to work with, and so is Eliza. She won't be here for ever, though, so you might well fill her shoes in time.'

Sally laughed. 'If I make it.'

'You'll make it.'

'You're very confident. How do you like your coffee?'

'White, no sugar.'

She rinsed out the only two mugs and made the coffee, then went back and joined him in front of the fire.

They talked more about the practice, and Sam told her about his training and his hospital experience, reducing her to tears of laughter with details of his howlers and exploits.

He was now twenty-nine, two years older than her

twenty-seven, and he'd only been a partner in the practice for a year.

That comforted her, because he seemed so confident and relaxed about general practice already. Maybe there was hope for her, too.

She told him about her training, her hopes and fears and disasters, and after a while they fell silent, with nothing but the hiss of the gas fire between them.

Their eyes met, and Sam took her cup and put it down on the hearth, then drew her gently down on to the rug beside him.

'I'm going to kiss you,' he told her, his voice deeper, husky.

She watched, mesmerised, as his head lowered slowly towards her. His eyes were open, glittering like bright blue flames, but as their lips met, his lids drifted down and a soft sigh rose in his throat.

His lips were tentative at first, seeking her permission in a gentle exploration that was totally unthreatening. They brushed and sipped and coaxed, until with a little sigh she opened to his persuasion and felt the velvet caress of his tongue.

She wasn't without experience, but nothing in her twenty-seven years had prepared her for the power of that first kiss.

Her blood seemed to sing in her veins, her heart pounding, and deep within her something wild and elemental came to life. Her arms crept round him, her fingers delving into his hair, and he shifted against her, bringing their bodies closer together.

Desire like white-hot arrows darted through her. With a shattered groan, Sam deepened the kiss, plundering her mouth again and again until she thought she would die of wanting him.

Finally, though, he lifted his head and stared down at her, his expression dazed. 'My God, Sally,' he said raggedly.

He lifted a trembling hand and smoothed her tangled hair away from her face. A gentle finger traced her lips, its touch wondrous, and moments later his lips replaced it, this kiss quite different from the last. It soothed where the other had inflamed, reassured and calmed her where the other had left her shaken and filled with longing.

He rested his head against hers, his arms still round her, holding her passively now as their passion stilled.

After a while he lifted his head and she met his eyes. A rueful smile touched his lips.

'I ought to go,' he said gruffly.

'Mmm.' She was beyond resisting him. If he tried to make love to her, she was powerless to stop him.

But he didn't. Slowly, reluctantly, he got to his feet and held out a hand to her, helping her up.

'Thanks for this evening,' she said unsteadily, remembering her manners at last, 'and thanks for waiting for me after your surgery.'

He grinned, a sexy, boyish grin that plucked her heart-strings.

'My pleasure,' he told her, and with one last, lingering kiss he left.

Two weeks later they were lovers, and within a year they were married and Ben was on the way.

Now, little more than eleven years later, they were back to square one.

Sam and Sally were working in the garden that Sunday afternoon when the hospital phoned to say that Fred Lucas had died. X-rays had shown that he had had

widespread cancer that had invaded almost all of his
lungs. The pneumonia had simply finished the job.

Sam had phoned the hospital a couple of times, and
as soon as he knew of the old man's death he went to
see Mrs Lucas at home.

'I knew he was done for weeks ago,' she told Sam
sadly. 'He was such a stubborn old fool, what with his
smoking and all. . .'

She broke off, sobs shaking her frail shoulders, and
Sam gathered her into his arms and held her while she
cried.

She didn't allow herself the luxury for long, straig-
tening up and dashing the tears from her cheeks with a
muttered apology.

'Let me get you a cup of tea,' she suggested, and
Sam was too aware of her loneliness to refuse. So he
stayed and drank two cups of tea and let her talk about
Fred and their life together and his stubborn ways, and
also his gruff kindness and patience with their grand-
daughter, the apple of his eye.

'Have you told your daughter yet?' he asked.

She nodded. 'Yes, they were there when he died.
They've gone back home now to pick up the babe, and
they're coming back here later. I think they're worried
I'll do something stupid.'

'And will you?' Sam asked gently.

She smiled, a sad, wistful smile. 'Oh, no. I've had
plenty of time to get used to the idea. To be honest,
there's a million and one things I've been putting off
because Fred wouldn't have liked me doing them. I
thought, once things settled a bit, I might work with
the WRVS for the Meals on Wheels. He didn't approve
of women doing things outside the home, but it isn't
always enough for everybody. Take your wife, for

instance. A clever girl like her's wasted shoving the vacuum round the floor all day.'

Sam nodded slowly. Mrs Lucas was right, Sally was clever and being trapped at home was killing her, as well as being a terrible waste of her talent.

He stood up. 'Talking of my wife, I suppose I ought to go home. Will you be all right now?'

'I suppose so,' she murmured. 'It'll take a bit of getting used to after all these years, but I'll keep busy, and I dare say I'll get used to it.'

'Call me if you need me—just for a chat, or to give you something to help you sleep—whatever. I'm always around.'

Mrs Lucas reached up and patted his cheek. 'Thank you, dear. You're very kind. I'm sorry I made a fool of myself.'

'Not at all. If you didn't cry I'd be much more worried about you.'

He stopped and brushed a kiss against her cheek. 'Take care, my dear. And don't forget, if you need me, call.'

'I will.'

He glanced back as he got in the car, and he saw her wave before the net curtain fell softly back into place, shielding her grief from prying eyes.

Sam drove thoughtfuly home. Poor old thing; all those years with that crabby old man and she could still manage to grieve for him. He must have shown her a different, more gentle side.

Nobody was really what they seemed, Sam mused. Take Sally, outwardly performing her role without complaint, inwardly seething with resentment.

Why hadn't she talked to him before?

Because, he realised, he hadn't been exactly receptive. He wasn't sure how receptive he was even now. The past week at home doing Sally's job had been a relief, really. He had been finding the pressure of the practice more and more difficult to deal with, and the mundane chores and mindless tasks were almost therapeutic.

Almost. The drama of the tumble-drier still lingered in his memory as a terrifyingly close shave, and the episode of the pansies was gone but not forgotten.

And he still, of course, had to manage to produce a meal they could all enjoy without reservation.

Even so, it was still a welcome change from the pressures of work, and he couldn't imagine why Sally was in such a hurry to abandon ship.

Perhaps the next two weeks would help to clarify things.

On Tuesday, Sally went to visit Jo Clarke and her new baby Thomas at home. Mrs Clarke's mother was there, and greeted Sally with a frown.

'Are you the doctor that worried my daughter to death?' she asked sternly.

Sally was a little taken aback. 'Not intentionally,' she told her. 'I was concerned, though, and did what I felt was right for the sake of the baby had there been a defect in his heart. I'm sorry you find my concern so difficult to accept. Would you rather I'd done nothing and the baby had suffered?'

The woman climbed down a little, a difficult task without losing face. 'I suppose you did what you thought was right,' she muttered. 'They're in here, but don't you tire them out.'

'I'm sorry, Mrs. . .?'

'Davis. Mrs Davis.'

'I'm sorry, Mrs Davis, but I think, if you don't mind, I'd like to see your daughter alone—and I believe you'll find her well-being is safe in my hands.'

And Sally shut the door firmly in the woman's face.

'Is she being a pain?' Jo Clarke asked softly.

'No, she's just very protective. I think she must have been very worried about you both.'

'Oh, don't—I was so scared that night, before they induced me. I managed to convince myself I would lose the baby, despite all they said to reassure me. The hospital were ever so good, but I was just so terrified.'

'I'm sure.' Sally perched on the chair near Jo and studied her with a smile. 'You look well enough.'

'Oh, I feel wonderful. It was a lovely easy delivery—much better than the first, and when they said he was all right, well—I think I nearly cried my eyes out!'

Sally smiled with her, then peered into the carry-cot beside the settee. 'He's a good big fellow, isn't he?'

'Three and a half kilos—nearly eight pounds, isn't it?'

'Something like that. I have to have a look at him, but I hate to wake him.'

'Don't worry,' his mother assured Sally, 'he's due for a feed any time now, so you can carry on. Just be prepared for his temper when you wake him and don't feed him!'

Sally laughed and turned back the bedclothes. He seemed tiny, little bent-up legs with tiny feet and toes, the nails like transparent shells. It brought so much back to Sally, the pain and the pleasure, the sleepless nights, the worry, not knowing how to cope with such an aggressively demanding little scrap.

Young Thomas Clarke opened his eyes then and stared at her, then let out a protracted wail.

'Sorry, little fellow,' Sally crooned, and examined him as quickly as she could.

'Do you want him now? He seems to be starving,' she said to Jo.

'Please. All that crying's got my milk pouring out!'

She quickly settled herself against the arm of the settee, and Sally scooped up young Thomas and laid him gently in his mother's arms.

Within seconds there was a blissful silence, broken only by the steady noise of his sucking.

'One happy baby,' Sally said with a smile. 'Well, he seems fine. I'm sorry I got you so worked up, but I really felt it was too important not to follow up.'

Jo laughed ruefully. 'That's all right. I know you acted for the best. I'm glad, really, because now it's over and he's fine and life can go on, you know? You don't want to pay any attention to Mum, though. She was frantic, and nothing I could say would calm her down. Actually,' Jo confided with a low laugh, 'she made me worse!'

Sally could well believe it. She made her goodbyes to Jo and baby Thomas, and managed to slip out of the front door without encountering the dreaded Mrs Davis again.

As she drove back to the surgery, she reflected on the vast differences between people; those who, like Mrs Davis, found fault in over-cautiousness, and others, like Sue Palmer and her husband, who actually thanked her for what Sally felt was bordering on negligence.

Thank God for variety, she thought, because otherwise it could be intolerable—especially if the world were made up of people like Mrs Davis!

She had another call to make that day, to David Jones, the man with shingles.

He was still in a lot of pain, so she increased his medication and gave him a mild sleeping-pill to take just for a few nights to see him through the worst.

'It's the crusts,' he said miserably. 'They seem to catch on things and when they lift off, it's as if they're attached to the nerve-endings.'

'Well, in a way they are,' Sally told him. 'That's why it can be such an acutely painful condition. You might be better not wearing anything on your top, just the sheet, so you haven't got things twisting round on you if you turn over in the bed.'

He nodded. 'I'll try that. Thank you, Dr Alexander. I'm sorry to be such a nuisance.'

'You're not a nuisance. I'm here to help,' she assured him.

It was a comforting thought that, for some of her patients at least, she was actually able to do something truly useful.

It was a long time since she'd felt really needed— except by her own children, of course, but that was rather different. This made her feel like a million dollars, and she breezed back into the surgery humming softly under her breath.

'Someone's happy,' a strange voice said, and she turned to see a man in a suit standing in the reception office. 'Dick Price,' he offered. 'Baker Pharmaceuticals. You must be Sam's wife.'

'That's right—Sally. What can I do for you?'

He grinned. 'Well, I had an appointment with Sam, but the ladies tell me he's bottled out and left you holding the baby.'

Sally laughed. 'Actually it's rather the other way round. Shall we go in my office?'

They chatted for a while, then he stood up to go, having left Sally some samples and various desk toys, notepads and other gismos.

She saw him out to his car and then headed for home herself. It was her evening off, and she was looking forward to a nice, quiet few hours in front of the television. Nothing demanding—perhaps a film or something light, or maybe they'd listen to music.

The work was getting to her. Not the amount, but the relentlessness of it, the fact of never having any time to herself, of having to fit in with other people all the time and do things to a structured timetable.

It was necessary, but after ten years out it was also foreign to her.

Deep in thought, she was driving along the quiet country road leading to their home when something glinted in the field below the road.

Odd, she thought. After a few more seconds she began to worry. It was probably nothing, but the road was high at that point, and there could easily have been something there—a car, for instance—which might have remained hidden for some time.

She pulled up and turned round, driving slowly back along the other side of the road.

Nothing.

She turned again and headed back towards home, and then she saw it—the edge of a car roof, the glass of the rear screen glinting in the low evening sun.

She pulled over and switched off the engine, climbed out of the car and headed towards the bank. She could see the car clearly now, half on its side, wedged in the angle of the bank.

'Hello?' she called, and as she listened she could hear the quiet hum of an engine.

She didn't hesitate another moment. Plunging down the bank, she ran round to the front of the car and peered in through the shattered windscreen.

A middle-aged couple were lying there, the man half-across the woman, who was dabbing ineffectually at blood oozing from his head. He was clearly unconscious, and she was trapped by his weight, unable to move.

Sally tapped on the windscreen. 'Open your window,' she yelled.

'I can't!' the woman called back. 'They're electric, and he's lying on the switches!'

'Open the sunroof, then!'

'I can't—my arm isn't long enough. I've tried.'

Sally looked around and found a hefty branch snapped off in their descent. She would have to smash the windscreen to turn off the engine, because there was an awful smell of leaking petrol and she had a nasty feeling.

'Cover your faces!' she shouted, and, swinging the branch, she knocked in the remains of the windscreen.

Glass went everywhere, but she ignored it, scrambling over the bonnet and reaching in to turn off the ignition.

The silence was wonderful, but Sally's relief was short-lived. The smell of petrol was getting worse, and she was terribly afraid she wouldn't be able to get them out in time.

'Are you hurt?' she asked the woman.

'No—no, I don't think so. Bernard's unconscious.'

'Yes, I can see. Keep talking to him, it might help him wake up.' She wasn't going to be able to reach the seatbelt buckles. That left only one alternative. 'I'm going to cut through your seatbelts with scissors,' she told the woman, 'and try and get you out. OK?'

The woman nodded and, wasting no time, Sally scrambled back up the bank, got the scissors out of her medical bag and headed back towards the bank. Then she turned back to her car, opened the doors and turned on her hazard flashers. Hopefully it would attract someone's attention. If only she'd been on duty, she would have had her mobile phone with her, but without it she was helpless.

She ran back down to the car and leant in through the windscreen.

'Are you sure you're not hurt?' she checked again with the woman.

'No, I'm fine, and Bernard seems to be coming round.'

Sally was relieved to hear it, because he was a big man and the thought of dragging him out over the dashboard single-handed and with untold injuries was too awful to contemplate.

So, unfortunately, was the idea of leaving them there to fry if the petrol suddenly went up.

'Bernard?' she yelled. 'Bernard, can you hear me?'

He moaned and opened his eyes, then shut them again with a groan.

'Bernard, listen, this is important. You've had a car accident, and you need to help me to get you out. Bernard, open your eyes!'

They fluttered, then opened again, this time more definitely.

'Who are you?' he asked hoarsely.

'My name's Sally Alexander—I'm a doctor. Bernard, I want you to tell me if you've got any pain anywhere apart from your head.'

He shifted a little, then shook his head carefully. 'No. Only my head and the odd twinge.'

'Can you feel your feet? Wiggle your toes.'

'They're fine.'

'Good. Right. I want you to help me. I'm going to cut through your seatbelt, and then I want you to try and climb out. The doors won't open, so you have to come out through the windscreen. OK?'

He closed his eyes. 'My head hurts like hell,' he muttered.

'I'm sure. Bernard, please help me. I don't want to worry you, but there's a strong smell of petrol and I want you both out of there fast.'

His head jerked up and he looked round at his wife. 'Louise? Are you all right?'

'Yes—please, Bernard, just get out like Sally says.'

He braced his arms against the lower door and Sally cut him free, then with a massive effort he pulled himself up and crawled carefully over his wife and out through the jagged opening.

'Louise, can you get out now?' Sally asked as soon as Bernard was clear.

'I'll try.' She fumbled with the seatbelt buckle, her fingers shaking like leaves, and then Sally leant in and helped her up and out.

'Right, let's get you well away from the car as quickly as possible,' she said to them both, and, with an arm round each of them, she hurried them over the uneven plough towards the bank.

'Get up there, away from the fumes,' she told Louise, and half pushing her, half dragging Bernard, she managed to get them to the top. As she did so, there was a deep boom from behind her and everything went black.

CHAPTER SIX

SAM was worried sick. Sally was due home early today, and here it was almost seven and still there was no sign of her.

He rang the surgery and spoke to Steve Dalton, the other partner, who was just leaving.

'No, haven't seen her for ages, Sam. She left about five with the Baker rep.'

Sam cradled the receiver with a crash and swore softly under his breath. Dick Price was an outrageous flirt, and the very last person he would have imagined Sally to go off with. So what the hell was she doing out so late with him?

Having dinner?

But he'd *made* dinner!

And, for once, it seemed possible that it might not be too awful.

So where the hell was she?

'Bloody hell!' he muttered.

'Daddy! You sweared!'

He turned and stared blankly at Molly's shocked little face.

'Sorry, darling. Have you done your homework?'

'Mmm-hmm. Can I have a sweetie?'

'OK.' Sally would kill him, but so what? If she was that worried about her kids, she'd be here, not out with that bloody fast-talking smoothie——

'Daddy! You're squashing me!'

He looked down at Molly's little hand crushed in his

99

big fist, and rubbed it gently, stricken. 'Sorry, darling. Did I hurt you?'

'Only a bit. Can I have two sweets?'

He laughed and ruffled her hair. 'I expect so. Where's Ben?'

'In the sitting-room watching a video.'

'Has he done his homework?'

Molly shook her head. 'Don't think so.'

Sam went into the sitting-room and left Molly foraging in the bag of sweets they had talked him into after school.

'Ben?'

His son jumped guiltily. 'Yes?'

'Have you done your homework?'

'I can't—I forgot my neat book.'

'So do it on a piece of paper and take it in, then you can copy it out tomorrow night.'

'That means doing it twice!' Ben protested.

Sam, unmoved, turned off the television. 'Tough. You should have thought of that when you left the book behind. Do it now, please.'

Ben's chin stuck out mutinously. 'Mummy wouldn't make me——'

'Well, too bad. Your mother isn't here. I am, and I'm making you. Now move it!'

Ben flounced past him, slamming the door and leaving Sam in a ringing silence.

His shoulders drooped. Where *was* she? It was no good trying the mobile; Steve had that with him as he was on duty.

He threw himself down on the settee and flicked on the television, catching the tail-end of the local news programme.

What if she'd had an accident? No. More likely Dick

Price had talked her into a meal and they were snuggled up in some intimate little restaurant somewhere having a cosy chat!

He made a conscious effort to relax, unfolding his fingers and watching as the blood flowed back into his white knuckles.

He'd kill her. The least she could have done was phone.

Well, sitting here wasn't achieving anything. He flicked off the television, jack-knifed out of the settee and went to find his stroppy son.

Maybe half an hour of Henry the Eighth would take his mind off Sally.

Sally turned into the drive and pulled up outside the garage. She could hardly move for weariness, but she forced herself to open the garage door and then drive the car in.

Her energy ran out at that point. Still shocked, she leant against the steering-wheel and gave a little sigh. She should have stayed at the hospital longer, but she knew Sam would be worried and she wanted to be at home.

It was silly driving. She'd told them she was taking a taxi, but had asked the taxi-driver to take her back to Sam's car and had driven home from there. It was only two miles, but she shouldn't have done it. She still wasn't thinking clearly, though.

She tried to summon the energy to open the car door and get out, but her legs were like jelly and so she sat there, her eyes glazed, and waited.

Sam would come soon, she knew. He'd help her.

Moments later her door was yanked open.

'About bloody time,' Sam growled.

She looked up. He was scowling, obviously livid, and she'd never been so pleased to see him in her life. 'Hi,' she murmured weakly.

'Hi?' he exclaimed. 'Is that the best you can come up with? Where the hell have you been? You might have phoned—damn it, woman, do you have any idea how late it is?'

She knew he was only angry because he'd been worried. It was an emotion she knew well. She tried to summon up a smile, but the effort was beyond her.

'I'm sorry. I didn't want to worry you but I couldn't get away. . .'

'Just tell him to go to hell. You're my wife, Sally—mine! Dick Price has no business keeping you out so late.'

'Dick Price?' She blinked and tried to concentrate. 'Who's Dick Price?'

Sam reached in and yanked her out of the seat, slamming her up against the side of the car. 'Don't play games with me, Sally! You know damn well who he is—you've just spent the entire evening with him!'

She shook her head. 'You're crazy,' she said weakly.

'Too bloody right I'm crazy! I love you! You're my wife—mine!' He searched her face. 'Did the bastard kiss you? Like this?'

His mouth swooped down, plundering her lips, forcing her head back against his arm as his tongue forced its way past her teeth, demanding entrance.

A sob rose in her throat, and he lifted his head glaring at her. 'Well?'

'You're mad,' she said blankly, and tears started at the corners of her eyes. 'Crazy. I've been at the hospital—a car went off the road and I pulled the occupants out just before it exploded. I was knocked out. I have't been with anybody.'

A puzzled frown crossed his face. 'But Steve said——

'Steve?'

'Dalton. Steve Dalton. He said you left with the pharmaceutical rep.'

She searched her memory, back into what seemed like the distant past. A face swam vaguely into her mind. 'Oh, him. He left at the same time, but we weren't together. I was on my way home when I saw a car in the ditch.'

Sam straightened away from her, his face pale. 'It exploded?'

She nodded, a shudder running through her.

'My God, Sally, you could have been killed!'

She started to shake uncontrollably, and with a muttered curse Sam scooped her up into his arms and carried her through into the sitting-room.

'Did they check you over?' he asked tersely.

'Mmm. I'm OK, just a bit shaken,' she told him unsteadily, and turned her face away. She couldn't seem to stop the tears, and crying always made her feel so vulnerable. The last thing she wanted was to be vulnerable when he was so angry with her.

She felt his hand curve gently round her cheek and turn her back towards him. 'Sally? Are you OK? Do you hurt? Darling, talk to me.'

She closed her eyes. 'I'm OK. Really. I just want to sleep.'

He let her go, settling her against the cushions, and in the background she could hear his voice on the phone.

Checking up on her, no doubt.

She was too tired to be angry with him, but later—
later she'd tell him what she thought of his suspicious
mind.

He could have trusted her. He should have done.
After all, she had trusted him in the same
circumstances.

But she was too tired now to deal with it. Much too
tired. Later, perhaps. . .

Sam sat on the other end of the settee, Sally's feet
against his thigh, and watched her sleep.

Apparently she was a heroine. According to the
nurse he'd spoken to, the A and E team had praised
her courage, the ambulance men said the couple would
have died without her help, the policeman first on the
scene was amazed that she had even seen the vehicle
from the road.

Sam felt dreadful. All evening he had harboured evil
thoughts, convinced she was out with Dick Price, when
all the time she had been risking her life to rescue
someone.

He thought of that kiss, savage, uncalled-for, totally
without sensitivity, and groaned.

Why, why, why had he done it?

Blind, unreasoning jealousy, of course. That was
what came of loving her.

Or not trusting her.

He winced inwardly. She was going to give him such
a hard time once she recovered. And, furthermore,
he'd deserve every last word of the tongue-lashing he
knew he had coming.

Ashamed, chastened, but above all concerned about
her, he leant over and took her hand.

'Sally?'

'Mmm?'

'Are you OK?'

She roused herself. 'Why do you care?' she mumbled.

He sighed. 'Because I love you,' he told her quietly. 'I know you're going to say I've got a funny way of showing it, but it's true.'

She sat up, pulling her feet away from him.

'You didn't trust me.'

He felt hot colour brush his neck. 'No. I'm sorry. I just know Dick Price's reputation. I also know how you feel about me at the moment. It wouldn't be unreasonable for you to spend the evening with him just for a bit of fun—a bit of light relief, someone to make you feel good about yourself.'

Her soft green eyes fixed him like bayonets. 'Do you really think I would do that when you were expecting me home for a meal? Without letting you know?'

He shifted uncomfortably. 'I've been late before without letting you know.

Her mouth tightened. 'I know. Aggravating, isn't it?'

She swung her legs over the edge of the settee and stood up, swaying slightly. 'I'm going to bed.'

'You need something to eat.'

'It would stick in my throat,' she told him flatly, and left him sitting there steeped in regret.

Sam wanted her to stay at home the next day, but she refused. She felt fine by the morning—a little sore from all the scratches on her legs and arms, but otherwise perfectly all right.

Anyway, she had no urge to sit around the house all day and look at the dirt. Sam was failing to get to grips with the housework, and today she was going to say something.

'I don't think you should go in,' Sam said again at breakfast.

'I'm fine. You just concentrate on cleaning the place up, and let me do my job.'

'My job,' he reminded her, piqued at the criticism.

'Not this week. This week it's mine, and you're doing this place—remember? I'll see you later—I'm on duty, so don't expect me.'

She kissed the children, but not Sam. As she went out, she heard Molly tell him off. 'Go and kiss her,' she said.

He followed her out. 'Molly says I have to kiss you.'

'Does she?' Sally said discouragingly. 'Tough.'

She arrived at the surgery at the same time as Steve Dalton.

'Hi,' he said breezily. 'Have a good evening?'

'No, I didn't,' she told him bluntly, 'and the next time anyone asks where I am, do me the service of getting your facts right. I was not with Dick Price—I was helping at the scene of an RTA and ended up nearly blown to bits and, let me tell you, I didn't appreciate getting yelled at by Sam when I got in because you'd got your facts wrong!'

She stormed into the building, leaving a confused and uncomfortable Steve open-mouthed in the car park.

He came in to see her after her morning surgery, bearing a cup of coffee and an apologetic grin. 'Sorry about that. I just caught a glimpse of you leaving the building together—I didn't think Sam'd go off at the deep end.'

'Well, it's high time you were less naïve,' she told

him. 'Is that for me, or are you just tormenting me with it?'

He handed her the coffee and perched on her desk. 'Actually I wanted to talk to you about David Jones—the chap with shingles? I had to go out to him at five this morning because he was in such pain and he'd already gone over his drug limit.'

'Oh, no. What did you give him?'

'IV diamorph, just to give him some peace, but I said you'd go back today as you're on duty and sort out something stronger—perhaps some sub-lingual Temgesic?'

'I don't like using such strong narcotics, but if he's in that much pain perhaps we need to.'

'Well, he certainly seems to be. You could try down the scale a bit with slow-release dihydrocodeine.'

'I'd rather,' Sally said thoughtfully. 'Oh, dear, I hope he doesn't end up with post-herpetic neuralgia.'

'Have you given him an antiviral?'

'Yes—almost before the rash appeared.'

'Oh, well, you can't do more than that,' he said, standing up and heading for the door. 'And I really am sorry if I messed things up with you and Sam.'

'Forget it,' she told him wearily. 'He'll get over it.'

So David Jones was suffering acutely still. Blast. And people always thought shingles was such a trivial illness. If only they knew.

She glanced at her watch. She'd better hustle—she already had several calls to make.

Downing the coffee, she picked up her bag and went out to the car, the mobile phone in her pocket. They really ought to have phones in the car all the time, she thought, as she headed off to her first call. Last night she could have got help much more quickly.

Luckily it had turned out all right, but it could so easily have gone badly wrong. . .

Sam looked round the house in despair. It was truly grim—dirt in every nook and cranny. He'd shoved the vacuum over the worst of it during the week, but somehow that didn't seem to show today.

It was the little things—the skirting-boards looked dusty, for instance, and the kitchen window was all splattered, not to mention the floor. And as for the bathrooms!

He'd never do it all to Sally's satisfaction, not if he spent a week on it. A thought occurred to him, and, picking up the Yellow Pages, he flicked through until he found what he was looking for.

Punching in the numbers, he waited a few seconds and then a brisk female voice came on the line.

'Good morning, Dustbusters. How can I help you?'

Sally didn't make it home for lunch. Instead she picked up a sandwich at a corner bakery and ate it between visits.

David Jones was suffering badly with his shingles, and she noticed that the rash was angry and rather reddened in one area, as it it had become infected. She gave him a prescription for a stronger painkiller and some antibiotics as well to counteract the infection, and told him to let her know if he needed her again.

He was obviouly getting depressed about the whole business, too. His wife was out at work all day and, with nothing to think about but his pain, the day must be very long.

'I could watch the telly, I suppose, but there isn't one in here.'

'You could go in the sitting-room,' Sally suggested.

'I suppose so.'

'Do you have a downstairs loo?'

He nodded.

'Well, then, rather than lying here and feeling miserable, would you be better on the sofa?' she asked. 'You could have a blanket over you, and then you'd have the television to distract you, or you could read.'

'Maybe tomorrow,' he said tiredly. 'Perhaps I'll sleep now you've given me these stronger pills.'

She left him with strict instructions to call if he needed her, and went back to the surgery.

As she walked in, Mavis signalled frantically to her and called her to the phone. 'Mrs Bailey—her daughter had an ear-ring stuck in her ear last week?'

Sally nodded. 'What's the matter?'

'She's been feeling ill—headache, nausea, et cetera. Her mother went to work and came back to find Carol unconscious.'

'Is that her on the phone now?'

Mavis nodded, and Sally took the phone. 'Mrs Bailey? Hello, it's Dr Alexander here. I gather Carol's unconscious; is that right? Can you rouse her?'

'No, not at all,' Mrs Bailey sobbed. 'She's like—dead!'

'Is she still breathing?'

'Breathing? Oh, yes, she is alive, but she won't wake up.'

'Right. Lie her on her side, so she can breathe properly, and I'll be right round. I'll ask one of the staff here to call an ambulance, so if you could give me directions, then I'll get round to you as soon as possible, all right?'

She scribbled down the directions, checked that

Mavis was calling the ambulance and ran. Ten minutes later she was kneeling by the side of the unconscious girl, examining a large reddened area behind her ear. Obviously she had failed to take the antibiotics and the infection had spread inwards, infecting the mastoid bone and possibly even causing a brain abscess. In any case, Carol was clearly very ill indeed.

'Is she going to be all right?' Mrs Bailey asked worriedly.

'I don't know—I hope so,' Sally told her, not wishing to dwell on the possible implications. 'Could you get a few things together for her?' That would keep her busy for a minute, anyway.

She had just inserted a cannula into a vein in Carol's forearm when the ambulance arrived, so she quickly wrote a letter to the admitting unit and handed it over as the men loaded Carol into the ambulance.

Sally watched as they pulled away, blue lights flashing, and with a sigh she went back to the surgery. She was hungry and thirsty—maybe she'd have time for a cup of tea before the phone rang again.

She found Mavis in the kitchen.

'Just brewing up, dear. Want one?'

Sally flopped into a chair with a sigh. 'Love one. Thanks.'

'How is she?' Mavis asked.

'Silly girl—she's really very ill. I took a butterfly clip out of her ear-lobe last week, and gave her a prescription for antibiotics, together with strict instructions to let it heal, but oh, no, she'd got another damned earring in, and the whole site was hugely inflamed and swollen. I suspect she's got a brain abscess.'

'Who has?' Martin Goody asked, walking in behind her.

'Carol Bailey—she's ignored an infected ear-lobe from a cheap ear-ring.'

'Not again! Sam saw her about that a few months ago. Well, maybe she's learned her lesson this time—if she lives.'

'If. Oh, well, she's out of our hands now.'

Martin pulled up another chair and sat down beside her. 'Busy day?'

She snorted. 'I'll say. I really could have done without it after yesterday.'

'I gather you were somewhat of a heroine.'

Sally flushed. 'I only did what anyone would have done. Anyway, how did you hear about it?'

'Sam rang to see how you were. He sounded concerned.'

'How touching.'

'Oh, dear.' Martin regarded her thoughtfully over the top of his mug. Mavis had left them, taking her tea back to her office, and they were alone. 'Things still bad, are they?'

Sally told him about Sam's behaviour the night before, leaving out the kiss, and Martin shook his head. 'Silly fool. Love clouds the judgement, of course.'

Sally snorted rudely. 'There wasn't much love in evidence at first, I can tell you! He was ready to kill me!'

'Jealousy. It's a terrible thing. I can tell you all about it, my dear. It wrecked my marriage.'

'But Jane was having an affair, I thought?' Sally said tentatively.

'Only after I'd driven her to it with my constant suspicion. I couldn't believe her when she told me that her boss was just a good friend. The thing was, *he* wanted to be more than that, and I could see it every time I saw them together. Jane couldn't, of course — not at first. He was very discreet, but it was obvious he loved her.'

'Is she happy with him?' Sally asked.

Martin shrugged. 'I suppose so. I don't really like to ask. I guess I don't want the truth.' He pushed back his chair and stood up. 'Forgive him for over-reacting if you can, Sally. He's only afraid of losing you. You can't expect him to be rational.'

She certainly couldn't, she thought. If nothing else, Sam had been irrational last night.

Draining her tea, she refilled the cup and took it with her into her surgery. It was five, time for her evening surgery, and doubtless there was a queue of patients backed up into the hereafter.

Did she really want to swap housework for this?

She chuckled to herself wearily.

No two ways about it, liberation was a two-edged sword. She was certainly beginning to see why Sam was always so tired and crabby these days, and for the first time in years, she was beginning to see the up-side of her own life.

She found she missed her friends, missed the camaraderie outside the school gates as they waited for the children to come out. She missed her health club, too — the lack of exercise was making her feel sluggish and flabby.

But she was enjoying being back in medicine, dealing with people's problems and trying to make their lives a little easier.

Did the two worlds have to be mutually exclusive?

If only there was a compromise. . .

*   *   *

Sam stood at the school gates waiting for the children. This was the part of the day he hated most—hovering on the fringe while the coven, as he called them, clucked and chittered like hens.

They threw him the odd glance, but so far no one had approached him—except Julia, the woman they shared Brownie-night lifts with, and she'd only wanted a favour.

He scuffed the toe of his trainer into the ground, kicking idly at a pebble. Whoever said sex discrimination was a thing of the past hadn't ever picked their kids up from school, he decided, because he was certainly discriminated against!

Of course he could always go over there and talk to them, but there'd be a pregnant silence as he arrived, and they'd all shuffle awkwardly.

No, he'd just stand here and wait, and hopefully Ben woudn't lose his trainers today, for a change.

He was tired, that was the trouble. Tired and crabby. The woman from Dustbusters had said they couldn't come until tomorrow, and so he'd had to make a start on the cleaning.

So far he'd done the sitting-room, and that was all. What a tip! Molly would kick up such a fuss if she knew what he'd chucked out, but the place was rapidly turning into a hovel. Sally should be pleased, though. It gleamed now from end to end—he'd even taken off the loose-covers and put them in the washing-machine.

They were in the new tumble-drier now. Please God it wouldn't catch fire, and he could get them back on before Sally got home. She'd be so pleased.

'But what happened to them, Sam?'
'I washed them—how was I to know they'd shrink?'

'Well, they don't normally. I put them on a fairly cool wash, tumble them on warm and put them back still damp—so what did you do?'

He flushed even deeper.

'They were filthy.'

'So?'

'So I gave them a hot wash.'

Sally sighed. 'And?'

'I tumbled them on hot.'

Sally shut her eyes. Men. How could they be so clever and yet so lacking in intelligence?

'Maybe if we damp them down and tug them on, they'll stretch,' she suggested, and Sam bundled them up and handed them to her.

'You do it—I've done quite enough damage.'

Two hours later the covers were back on—just about—and Sally was curled up in the drawing-room on a dry sofa with a cup of tea.

Sam was sitting opposite, his jaw set, looking like a thundercloud.

'Sam?'

'Everything I try and do goes wrong,' he said bitterly. 'Every last damn thing.'

'You're just not naturally domesticated, darling,' she told him.

He snorted rudely. 'You knew that when you married me.'

'Hey—when we got married, I wasn't domesticated either!'

He gave a wry grin. 'No, you weren't, were you? We had some rum meals those first few months.'

'It was fun, though.'

His face softened with the memories. 'Yes—yes, it

was fun. What happened to us, Sally? Where did we go wrong?'

'I don't know,' she said truthfully. 'I really don't.'

He swirled his mug, staring down into the dregs of the tea. 'Are you enjoying being back at work?'

Her smile was wry. 'More than you're enjoying my job, I fancy.'

He snorted. 'That isn't difficult. Of course, if I could do it well it might have its own reward.'

'I shouldn't bet on it,' she advised him drily. 'I'm going to ring ITU and find out how Carol Bailey is. They were scanning her.'

Sam followed her, propping his hips against the worktop beside her and listening to the conversation.

'Craniotomy to drain a small abscess in the brain, eh? You were right—clever girl.'

Sally laughed. 'Sam, you'd have to be blind and ignorant not to get that right—she had all the right symptoms. I wonder if she'll make a complete recovery, or if she'll be left with epilepsy?'

'God only knows. Why don't you come to bed while the phone's quiet——?'

'You were saying?'

She lifted the receiver. 'Dr Alexander.' She listened for a moment, then scribbled an address. 'Yes, of course I'll come.'

She gave Sam a weary smile. 'Don't wait up.'

CHAPTER SEVEN

THERE'S a time, towards the quiet morning, when we are at our most vulnerable, when our souls most readily slip the leash.

At just before four, Sally was woken by the phone. At her own lowest ebb, she felt her blood chill even further as the man spoke.

'I can't wake her—she's freezing, and she won't talk to me!'

'I'll come. Give me your address,' she said calmly. Jotting down the directions, she watched as Sam got out of bed, laid her clothes out ready on the bed and then waited quietly until she put the phone down.

'What is it? You look awful.'

'He can't wake his wife—he sounded awfully young, Sam—in his twenties?'

She dressed quickly without saying any more. Sam waved her off, and then she was on her own. What would she find? A coma? Death, even? And from what? Suicide? Brain haemorrhage? Heart attack?

God knows, she thought, and wondered what on earth she was doing. She was qualified, of course, but equipped? Emotionally and spiritually, did she have what she would need to deal with the situation and help those left behind?

She arrived at the house to find lights on from top to bottom and the front door hanging open.

A man of about thirty ran out, clad only in pyjama bottoms, his face ravaged.

116

'Oh, Dr Alexander, thank God you're here. Help her, please—she's upstairs.'

Sally followed him in, running lightly up the stairs and into the bedroom.

His wife was lying in the bed, looking very young and quite peaceful. She was also obviously dead.

As Sally examined her briefly, something else became obvious. She was pregnant.

'Has she been complaining of anything in the last few days? Any pain? Headaches, that sort of thing?'

'She had a headache yesterday.'

That could well be significant, Sally thought, because, whatever she'd died of, she hadn't been able to get help. Either that, or hadn't wanted to. There was still the possibility of suicide. Certainly on brief examination there was nothing to indicate the cause of death. She straightened up slowly.

'What's wrong with her?' Mr Lennard asked frantically. 'Why aren't you doing anything?'

Sally folded her stethoscope and put it in her pocket. 'Mr Lennard, I'm awfully sorry, I'm afraid your wife's dead. She's been dead for some time.'

He stared at her blankly for several seconds, then his eyes swivelled to his wife. He shook his head slowly. 'No. No, she can't be—she can't!'

He fell on his knees beside her, grabbing her shoulders and shaking her, yelling at her to wake up.

Gradually the yells turned to sobs, then he rested his head against her and wept.

Sally left him to it, checking the other bedrooms to see if there were any children asleep in the house. There weren't, thank God. She didn't feel up to dealing with them. He was going to be quite enough of a challenge.

She went down to the kitchen and put the kettle on. While it boiled she looked round, to see if she could discover any clues. The kitchen was neat and tidy, well-kept, as if Mrs Lennard had been well up to last night. Certainly there was no evidence of her having been ill at all.

She checked the bin for pill bottles, but there was nothing obvious. The police would have to investigate, of course, but so far Sally could see nothing suspicious. She would have to check the woman's medical records to see if there was any reason why she might have died—high blood-pressure leading to a brain haemorrhage, for instance—but the post-mortem would reveal the cause of death.

Oh, dear. She rang the police, gave them the address and went back up to Mr Lennard.

He was still kneeling by his wife, his face ravaged with pain and now the knowledge that, yes, she was dead. He had gone through disbelief into belief, and the next stage was shock.

Sally laid a hand gently on his shoulder.

'Mr Lennard? Is there anyone I can call for you? Anyone you want to tell?'

He looked slowly up at her, his brows drawn together in confusion. 'Tell?' he said hoarsely.

'Your parents, perhaps? Your wife's parents?'

'Oh—um—I suppose. . . My mum. . .' His voice cracked, and she laid an arm round his shoulders and hugged him reassuringly.

'Come on—come downstairs and have a cup of tea and I'll help you phone.'

He was reluctant to leave his wife, but Sally persuaded him to come down to the kitchen and pressed a cup of hot, sweet tea into his hand.

'Drink this,' she told him.

'I hate sugar in tea.'

'Just drink it. You can have the next one straight.'

'Gabby always has sugar in tea,' he said, and then he started to cry again, huge racking sobs that shook his body mercilessly.

Sally took the tea out of his hand and put it on the table, then stood beside him, her hands resting on his shoulders.

His arms came round her waist and he buried his face in her front and cried his heart out.

That was how the police found them a few minutes later.

A policewoman went upstairs to check the bedroom, while her male colleague tried to get some sense out of Mr Lennard about his wife's details.

'Have any of the dead woman's relatives been informed?' he asked Sally.

She shook her head. 'No, we were just getting round to that.'

'Leave it to us,' he advised her. 'We'll send a patrol car round. There'll have to be a post-mortem of course.'

Mr Lennard shuddered. 'No,' he pleaded weakly. 'Oh, no. . .'

'I'm sorry, sir, but we have to establish the cause of death.'

He flinched at the word, and Sally reached out automatically to comfort him.

The police procedure seemed to take forever, and it was six o'clock before Sally was able to get away.

Sam was up and dressed, waiting for her when she got home.

'Was she dead?'

Sally nodded. 'Yes. It was awful. She's pregnant. . .'
Sally's voice cracked, and she found herself in Sam's
arms, wrapped hard against his chest. She didn't want
to cry. She ought to be able to deal with this sort of
thing without crying. It happened every day. Why was
she finding it so damned hard to deal with?

Her tears fell faster, and Sam rocked her gently
against his chest and made soothing noises, meaning-
less sounds of comfort that gradually calmed her.

She straightened away from him, scrubbing the tears
from her cheeks, and looked round the kitchen.

'Any tea?' she asked unevenly.

'I'll make some—sit down.'

He switched the kettle on. It boiled very quickly, as
if he'd been expecting her.

'Was it Gabby Lennard?' he asked.

'Mmm.'

'What a damn shame. Any idea why?'

'No. . .Was she hypertensive?'

'Slightly. I was going to monitor it closely—actually
she was due in this afternoon for an ante-natal check.'

'Oh, God.'

Sam put a cup of tea down in front of her, turned a
chair round and straddled it, folding his arms along the
back and regarding her steadily.

'Awful, isn't it? Such a wicked waste.'

'I'm sorry I cracked up,' she said in a low voice. 'It
was just having to be strong for him, and deal with the
police as if it was just an inanimate object we were
talking about instead of a young, apparently healthy
pregnant woman. . .'

She broke off, on the brink of tears again, and took
a gulp of her tea.

'Don't apologise,' he said softly. 'We all cry when it's too bad. I'd be appalled if you didn't.'

She looked up at him, amazed. 'When have you ever cried?'

He laughed softly. 'Me? I'm the world's original marshmallow.'

'I've never seen you cry about a patient.'

He shrugged. 'I don't bring it home. I don't think it's fair to you, but that doesn't mean it doesn't affect me.'

'You do bring it home,' Sally told him gently. 'When you're crabby and irritable, yell at the kids—there's usually something that's gone wrong. You just don't bring your vulnerable part home. You should. It would make you easier to love.'

He regarded her thoughtfully over the back of the chair. 'Am I so difficult to love?' he asked softly.

She sighed. 'No, not always. Sometimes you're all too easy to love.'

His eyes softened, and his jaw clenched as if he was fighting his feelings. Sally smiled tentatively.

'Of course you *can* be downright impossible—like when jealousy has a grip on you, for instance.'

He flushed slightly. 'I don't know how to apologise for that. I was a complete pig.'

She nodded. 'Yes, you were. I've been thinking about that.'

She took a swig of her tea and set the mug down again.

Sam was watching her guardedly. 'Yes?' he prompted.

'I think we ought to have car phones. Then we'd be in contact all the time, not just on duty. If I'd had a car phone the other night, I could have got help straight away.'

He gave a wry grin. 'Funny, that. I've been thinking the same thing, but I didn't know how to suggest it because I thought you'd feel I was trying to keep tabs on you.'

'So why shouldn't you? Sam, I have nothing to hide.'

He sighed. 'I know that. I just thought you might feel—I don't know—threatened.'

She smiled patiently. 'Sam, I don't feel threatened because you love me. I just don't like being strong-armed out of the car and kissed until my lips are bruised!'

He rubbed his hands over his face. 'Oh, dear. That's going to take some getting away from, isn't it?'

'Mmm. You'll have to work terribly hard to make it up to me.'

He gave a rueful laugh. 'I have been—hence the loose-covers.'

She laughed. 'Yes, well. . .'

'Don't say a word! Don't say a single damn word!'

Sally bit down on her smile, finished her tea and then went to shower and change for the day.

As the water streamed over her, she reflected on his confession that he did sometimes cry about patients. It was something she hadn't realised, a chink in his armour that made him somehow all the more lovable.

She began to feel that things might, after all, work out between them—but only if they didn't slip straight back to square one as soon as their roles were reversed again. . .

She told Martin Goody all about Gabby Lennard as soon as she arrived at work.

'Oh, dear, how sad. Have you checked the notes?'

'No, I'm just about to,' she said. She pulled the

envelope of Mrs Lennard's details out of the drawer and removed the contents. 'Slight hypertension—one-forty over ninety-five. There's a note here from Sam to follow up and watch for complications, but there were none present at the last antenatal check, by all accounts, and she wasn't on an antihypertensive. He was obviously happy just to keep an eye on her.'

Martin nodded thoughtfully. 'That's just what I would have done. The notes are very thin—she's obvously been quite a well person. How did her husband take it?'

'He was pole-axed. Young, healthy couple on the brink of becoming a family—how would you expect him to feel?'

'Hmm. How do you feel?'

Sally gave him a weary smile. 'Awful. I howled all over Sam.'

'Good. We all need someone to howl all over when things like this happen. I must say I've been known to howl on Sam, too!'

Sally stared at him in amazement. 'You?'

'Oh, yes—occasionally, when it just seems all too unfair and sad. It's mutual. I've mopped Sam up in the past—well, you must have done, too.'

'No. He never brings it home—well, not like that. I get the temper and the distraction, just not the vulnerable bit. I thought he'd grown hard.'

'Sam?' Martin was clearly amazed. 'Sam's a pussy-cat. Things rip him to bits—that's why he's so conscientious. And being slightly understaffed, as we are, there isn't time to get away and top up as much as we probably should. Actually I should imagine being at home is doing him a power of good.'

Sally thought of the pansies, the tumble-drier and

the loose-covers. 'Not entirely,' she said with a chuckle. 'I think he's finding the odd challenge there, as well.'

'Do him good,' Martin grinned. 'After all, that's what you want, isn't it? For him to struggle a bit?'

She sobered. 'Not struggle, exactly, Martin—just see it from the other side. I've got more insight into his life now. I'd forgotten about the emotional pressure. I thought I'd find the new drugs and so on difficult, but actually it's the age-old problem of dealing with sad, sick people that's the challenge and the reward.'

Martin nodded. 'Are you enjoying it?'

'Enjoying? I'm not sure that's the word, but certainly I feel more alive than I have in years, even without any sleep!'

'You look well. Happier, more relaxed.'

'Hmm. I just hope it lasts once this little game of ours is over and we settle back into our rut.'

'You'll have to make sure that doesn't happen, won't you?' Martin said over his shoulder. 'I'm going to tackle my paper-work before the patients arrive.'

Paper-work. Now that was one part of the job that Sally was definitely *not* enjoying!

Sam slowed the treadmill to a walk then, after cooling off for a minute, he turned it off and went over to the heart monitor. A hundred and fifteen, and falling. That was more like it. He was jogging up to fifteen minutes now at seven miles an hour—not up to Sally's standard, but yesterday he had tried the course and pushed himself a bit too hard.

Still, it was progress.

Amy approached him with a smile. 'You're doing really well.'

He gave her a wry grin. 'After a rather shaky start.

Amy, I wanted to ask you something—is the aromatherapist around today?'

'Yes, she's here now.'

'Does she have anybody with her? Only I'd like to talk to her, if she's got time.'

'I'll tell her. Why don't you go and change and I'll see what I can do?'

'Thanks.'

'My pleasure.'

He showered and changed, then went up and found Amy in conversation with a woman in a white tracksuit.

She was softly pretty, a delicate blonde with eyes that saw everything. No doubt she could help him, but Sam realised at once he wouldn't get away with less than a full confession.

'Hi. I'm Laura. Why don't you come into my office so we can talk?' she said, and led Sam through a doorway into a small room decorated in restful blues and greens. There was a wonderful scent in the air, and he breathed deeply and felt himself unwind.

She perched on her chair, waved to another and smiled. 'Now, what can I do for you?'

There was no point in beating around the bush. 'Um—I was reading an article about aromatherapy in one of my medical journals the other day. They said something I found interesting.'

'About the therapeutic effects of essential oils?'

He grinned awkwardly. He could feel the colour beginning to climb up his neck. Damn, why was it so difficult to talk about something so normal?

'Actually, no—it was about aphrodisiacs.'

'Ah.' Laura sat back in her chair. 'Are you having problems?'

'No! That is—not exactly. Well, yes, in a way.'

Laura waited patiently while he floundered, growing more acutely embarrassed by the minute. Hell, why had he started this?

'Is your marriage in a rut?' she suggested after he'd finally run out of non-explanations.

He sighed with relief. 'Yes. Exactly. We've lost touch with each other. We're dealing with it, but I just thought, if I could woo her back. . .' He shrugged diffidently. 'I love her. I just can't seem to reach her any more.'

'Does she love you?'

He sighed. 'I don't know. I hope so. Maybe. I messed up the other night, went totally over the top when she was late home. I think that rather nobbled any progress I might have made.'

'Oh, dear. You mustn't get so worked up. Stress is very bad for you, you know.'

He looked at Laura, calm, beautiful, absolutely relaxed, and sighed. 'I know. I'm not very good at dealing with it, either.'

'You should work on it. In the meantime, I can give you an aphrodisiac massage oil that will blow her socks off. That do you?'

He laughed softly. 'It sounds wonderful.'

She went into another room and came back a few moments later with a small bottle of oil.

'What's in it?'

'Jasmine and ylang-ylang in a neutral base oil. You don't need much.'

He paid her, indifferent to the hideous expense, and slipped it into his pocket.

'You can put it in bath-water, sprinkle it on bedding or use it as a massage oil, but you must be careful with mucous membranes and eyes; it can sting a little. Oh, just one other word of warning——' she grinned mischievously '—it'll blow your socks off, too.'

Sam gave a wry grin. 'That won't take much doing at the moment.'

Laura smiled. 'Have fun.'

'Thank you.'

He shook her hand, surprised at the strength of it, and then went home to plan his assault.

Dustbusters were coming, and they would make the place presentable. That would help. So would a nice meal.

Sally was beginning to soften, he knew it. She was emotionally vulnerable after Gabby Lennard's death, and tonight she would be tired and achy—just ready for a long hot bath followed by a nice, soothing massage.

Not that he would let it lead anywhere—not yet. He was beginning to realise that the only way to woo her was to tease and torment, slowly driving her out of her mind.

He used to do it years ago, when they worked together—brushing against her, the odd touch, the veiled promise.

It used to leave her gasping.

He chuckled. It had worked the first time—after a fortnight of gentle teasing and winding her up, she had been more than ready when he finally made love to her.

And so had he. That, too, had blown his socks off.

He closed his eyes for a moment, the memory sweet and sharp in his mind.

She had been so shyly eager, so full of curiosity. And that first shattering climax of hers—the little cries, the soft gasping breaths, the way she had clung to him. . .

Desire stabbed him now, leaving his knees weak and his heart racing. This was going to kill him, but he was going to do it.

He wouldn't make love to her tonight, even if she begged him.

Well, perhaps if she begged. . .

Compared with the trauma and tragedy of the night, the rest of that day was relatively quiet and peaceful. Sally worked steadily through her surgeries and the antenatal clinic, trying hard not to think about Gabby Lennard who should have been there for a routine check-up.

She wondered what the PM result would show, if anything. The police certainly weren't ruling out suspicious circumstances, but they seemed fairly confident that her death was due to natural causes.

Her evening surgery was over promptly, for a change, and she arrived home at six-thirty to find Sam and the children in the kitchen doing a wordsearch in one of Ben's puzzle books.

'You're early,' Sam said, and she felt the warmth of his smile right down to her toes.

She bent and kissed his cheek. 'Want a hand with the supper?'

'No, it's all under control. You go and change into something sloppy and sit with the kids, and I'll make you a cup of tea.'

It sounded a wonderful idea. She was tired and achy after her sleepless night, and the thought of slopping around in an old tracksuit while Sam waited on her was blissful.

She went upstairs and was staggered at how clean

and tidy everything looked. Sam must have worked like a Trojan!

She pulled on an old jogging suit and went back downstairs.

There was a cup of tea waiting on the table, and through the open utility-room door she could see a pile of ironing neatly folded on the worktop beside the ironing board.

Good Grief! He can't have sat down for a moment!

Molly snuggled up to her side. 'I found "rabbit",'she told her, pointing to the wordsearch. 'We're looking for "anteater"—Daddy couldn't find it either.'

She looked up at Sally, clearly expecting her to find the word.

Goodness knows how. She could hardly see, never mind concentrate.

'I don't know,' she began, and there, miraculously, it sprang out of the jumble of letters at her. 'Here it is, it's diagonally and backwards.'

Even Ben looked impressed. If the truth be told, Sally was pretty impressed herself. Smugly, she sipped her tea and found "giraffe", then winked at Sam over the children's bent heads.

'Creep,' he mouthed, and she giggled. One-upmanship was very childish, but tonight she needed to play silly games.

There had to be a balance.

She wondered how Mr Lennard was coping with the shock of losing his wife and baby so suddenly. She looked at her children's bent heads, and tears welled in her eyes.

'Stop it,' Sam told her softly. 'You've done your bit. Let it go.'

She nodded, dragging in a deep breath, and picked up her tea.

'You've been very busy,' she said, glancing round and catching sight of the ironing again.

He grinned, a lopsided, rueful smile. 'Actually, I have a confession. I got Dustbusters in to deal with it.'

She laughed. She didn't mean to, but the whole irony of the situation hit her.

'I think I'll have a day off tomorrow, too,' she said between chuckles. 'I'll get a locum in.'

'It's hardly the same,' he protested, looking deeply hurt.

Then she caught the twinkle in his eye and laughed again.

'You're a cheat, Sam Alexander. A miserable, wretched cheat.'

'But I did it for you,' he said, throwing her a winning smile and pulling a casserole out of the oven. 'Come on, kids, clear the table. Time for supper.'

'Is that that Marks and Spencer casserole you got today?' Molly asked ingenuously.

Sally bit her lips to keep the laughter in, but failed dismally.

Sam struggled, but then succumbed. 'Little rat,' he muttered. 'I thought I'd got away with that one.'

Sally was too hungry to care. She cleaned her plate, as did the children and Sam, and then they tucked into a very definitely bought chocolate gâteau and cream.

'Another little number I knocked up this afternoon,' Sam said without apology as he dished it up.

'Daddy! You're telling porky-pies again!' Ben said cheerfully.

'Yes, inferior role-modelling, darling,' Sally teased.

Sam harumphed. 'You don't have to have any if you don't want it.'

She guarded her plate with her arm. 'I must say,' she said as she licked her spoon thoughtfully clean of every last scrap, 'our housekeeping budget is going to rocket if we go on like this.'

'Even you buy chocolate gâteau!'

'Mmm. But I do the ironing myself.'

Sam grinned. 'You want everything to have a brown mark this shape in the middle?' He drew an iron in the air, and Sally shrugged her defeat.

'I rest my case,' Sam said with finality.

'Oh, that's wonderful. . .'

'It's meant to be. You're very tense.'

Sam's hands smoothed up her back, his fingers working the taut muscles of her shoulders before gliding down her arms.

It was luxury. She'd just crawled out of a deliciously scented bath, to be greeted by Sam dressed only in a towel, telling her to lie on the bed.

A huge fluffy towel was stretched out on her side, and she took off her dressing-gown and lay face down on the bed.

She felt shy in front of him, strangely, even after all these years. Maybe because she knew she couldn't fool him any more, or maybe because she knew things were different now between them.

Certainly there was something different about Sam, a new playfulness she hadn't seen for years.

His hands felt so good on her. They always had, right from the beginning. Even recently, when she'd been angry, his touch had never been repellent.

Now, though—his hands slid lower over her ribs,

teasing the outer margins of her breasts, making them ache for his touch.

He moved down, over her legs, sitting by her feet and working deeply into her thighs, smoothing and kneading, his touch hypnotic.

He moved her legs apart slightly, his hands encircling each thigh in turn, his touch sure and confident.

He worked down her calves, into her feet, between her toes even—the tension evaporated away like mist on a sunny morning.

'Turn over,' he commanded softly.

She was shy now. Facing him, somehow, was different.

She did as she was told, though. She just kept her eyes shut.

He worked on her face and neck, carefully avoiding her eyes, and then down over her collarbones, down each arm to the fingertips then back up again, then he dribbled more oil on his hands and spread it smoothly, evenly over her breasts.

Her breath caught. What was he doing? His touch was different now, lighter, less purposeful. She felt her nipples peak, and he rolled them gently between finger and thumb. She arched up, a soft cry coming from her lips, and he smoothed down over her ribs, his hands working lightly over the softness of her abdomen.

His palms slid over her hips, down, round, his fingers teasing the soft, damp curls as he came round again to stroke up, over her ribs.

Desire, sharp and sweet, pooled low in her body. She wanted him—needed him, in a way she hadn't needed him for years.

A shudder ran through her, and she heard Sam's low grunt of satisfaction. He lifted her right leg, propping it against his chest and sliding his hands down her thigh almost to the apex, then back up again, round and back, round and back.

She arched her hips towards him but he ignored her, taking her other leg and giving it the same treatment.

He worked his way down to her feet, paying particular attention to the sensitive area behind her knees and on the top of her foot, then suddenly he was gone.

She felt the bed shift, and he tugged the towel out from under her.

She heard him washing his hands and cleaning his teeth, then he came back into the bedroom, slid under the covers and flicked out the light.

'Night, darling,' he said softly. 'Sleep well.'

She lay open-mouthed for a moment, stunned. He couldn't do that to her! She was aching with need, desperate for the feel of his body united with hers. . .

A low groan erupted from her lips, and she turned into the pillows and squeezed her eyes tight shut. Her body throbbed, every heartbeat echoed in her secret core. She needed him, the evil rat, and he knew it!

Frustration burned at her for a while, but then a slow smile played around her lips. So he was up to those tricks again, was he? Well, two could play at that game.

She just hoped he was ready for it, because when they finally stopped playing with fire, there was going to be a hell of a conflagration!

CHAPTER EIGHT

SALLY phoned up for the result of the post-mortem on Gabrielle Lennard on Friday afternoon.

The result was conclusive and in its way a relief. She had died of a cerebral haemorrhage because a tiny cherry aneurism, like a little bubble, had burst deep inside her brain. She must have had it for years, and the slight rise in her blood-pressure due to pregnancy had been just enough to burst it.

It was one of those things that, without such an event, would normally have remained undetected unless it was revealed in a CT scan for another problem. It was quite unavoidable, there was nothing that could have been done and so Sally was able to go and see the woman's distraught husband and tell him that.

It might stop him blaming himself too much for not having woken earlier, or worried about her headache sooner, or any of the myriad things bereaved people found to flagellate themselves with, Sally thought.

Gabby's parents were with him, sitting sadly in the kitchen where Sally had comforted him the day before, and they seemed glad of the opportunity to discuss the cause of her death and the inevitability of it.

They had been to see her at the hospital before the post-mortem, and had accepted her death, although not the necessity for it. Sally's words seemed to give them a measure of acceptance, although she knew anger would come later.

She went home to Sam and found him in the kitchen putting a chicken in the oven.

'I wish the kids would eat something else,' he said, looking at the chicken with disfavour. 'They didn't even like the garlic-basted one we had the other day for a change.'

She tried to summon a smile, but it wouldn't come.

'Ah, love,' he said, his face registering understanding, and, opening his arms, he folded her hard against his chest.

'I've just seen Gabby Lennard's husband and parents,' she mumbled into his shirt-front.

'Did you get the PM result?'

She nodded. 'Cerebral aneurism.'

'Oh, hell. Well, I suppose it was quick.'

Sally eased out of his arms and filled the kettle for something to do. 'She was just so damned young—only twenty-six.'

'Some people go when the time's right, like old man Lucas. Some hang on beyond what they and their relatives can bear, often suffering far more than seems fair. Others, like Gabby, are snatched way before their time.'

She nodded. 'That's what it feels like—that it just wasn't her time, but I suppose it was. It was perfectly natural—just a congenital defect in the artery wall.'

'Still hard to take.'

'Mmm.' She emptied the teapot and rinsed it out. 'Where are the children?'

'Cubs and Brownies. Julia took them. I said I'd pick them up.'

'I'll go, if you like. I could do with seeing the other mums.'

'Your coven? I expect they've missed you.'

She smiled wanly. 'I've missed them. There really isn't time for a social life, is there? The times I've called you antisocial, but there's just nothing left, is there? No time and no energy.'

He pulled her into his arms and hugged her. 'Only a week to go. If you want to give up, we can always swap back at any time.'

She pushed him away gently. 'No fear. Just tough it out, Mrs Mop.'

He gave a wry grin. 'Am I really so transparent?'

She snorted. 'Just a touch. I'll go and change, then I'll pick up the children. Could you make a pot of tea?'

He tugged his forelock. 'Yes, Mum. Certainly, Mum.'

'That's it—a little deference to the breadwinner, please.'

He made a rude noise, and with a laugh she ran up the stairs to their bedroom.

The lingering scent of jasmine and ylang-ylang hung on the air, sweet and provocative.

She closed her eyes, remembering the sensuous glide of his hands over her skin. Her pulse quickened, and little stabs of desire pierced her.

It would be interesting to see how this game of his was to be played—and to see if she would be capable of playing it without breaking the rules and grabbing him before the final whistle!

She was on duty that weekend from Saturday lunchtime to Monday morning, a fact which irked her in the extreme. It was a wonderful weekend, the weather glorious. It seemed fitting that Saturday was April Fools' Day, because if she hadn't challenged Sam she could have been out in the garden getting to grips with the rising tide of spring.

Instead she just had time to stroll round it and weep with exasperation in between calls. If only Sam could be trusted, she thought, and then remembered her pansies.

Perhaps everything could wait. It was only another week, after all.

She found herself looking forward to the end of that next week more and more as the weekend went on. Most of the calls were spectacularly insignificant—but she knew Sam almost never refused to visit a patient, and so she felt she should do the same, just to gauge how irksome it could be.

She found out, in spades.

By Sunday afternoon she was ready to tell the next caller to drop dead, but when the call came in she was very much afraid that he might.

'Man of forty, severe chest pain—a Mr Turner,' she told Sam as she ran for the car. 'I'll see you later.'

She arrived at the house to find a boy in his mid-teens waiting anxiously at the side of the road.

'Are you the doctor?' he asked, and when she confirmed it he all but dragged her through the house into the garden.

'Dad's here,' he told her, and led her to the shade under an apple-tree. A man was lying there, his skin grey and clammy, his lips bluish, and a woman, obviously his wife, was smoothing his brow and talking calmly to him.

'Oh, thank God you're here,' she said fervently to Sally.

She knelt down beside the man. 'What's his name?' she asked.

'Brian.'

'Brian,' Sally said, 'it's Dr Alexander. Can you hear me?'

He grunted affirmation.

'Can you tell me where the pain is?'

'Chest,' he mumbled. 'Weight—and my arm.'

'When did it start?'

'Digging. Rested for a bit—better—did some more. Bad now. . .' He broke off and licked his lips, obviously in great pain.

'Brian, I'm going to sit you up a bit, see if that eases it. Don't move, I'll get something to lean you on.'

She looked round the garden and saw a solid wooden chair.

'That'll do. Turn it upside down and he can lean on the back. He'll need cushions, ' she told his family, and they rushed to follow her instructions, clearly only too glad to do something useful.

She asked his wife to help sit him up, and the son pushed the chair up behind him and arranged the heap of cushions so that he could lean comfortably back on it.

'Better?'

He nodded. His speech was still slurred, but clearer than before. 'I can breathe better—as if some of the weight's gone.'

'Good. I'll give you something for the pain while we wait for the ambulance. OK?'

She put a cannula in his hand ready for drugs at the hospital, and gave him diamorphine for the pain.

Because of its importance in reducing risk of a further attack if given within six hours of the pain, he was likely to be given a thrombolytic drug on arrival at the hospital. The sooner it was given, the better, but just for good measure she gave him half an aspirin tablet to start the process.

She had a defibrillator in the car, but she was hoping she wouldn't need it. He looked reasonably stable, and his colour had improved slightly since they had sat him up. Happy that he was in good shape for the ambulance transfer, she sent the son out to the front of the house to wait for the ambulance.

'He will be all right?' Mrs Turner asked softly.

'I hope so,' Sally said, unwilling to reassure blindly when things could still go wrong. She was also very conscious of the fact that Brian was probably listening, even though the diamorphine had made him very drowsy. 'I think he's had a bit of a heart attack,' she said simply. 'They'll be able to tell you more at the hospital when they've done some tests.'

'Oh, dear. Oh, I feel so guilty. I nagged and nagged him about that digging. . .' She started to cry, and Sally squeezed her shoulder and thought of how much pressure Sam was under. He and Brian were about the same age, she reflected uncomfortably, and suddenly she couldn't wait to get home to him and just tell him how glad she was that he was alive.

The ambulance came, and Brian Turner and his wife and son were loaded into it, then Sally made her way home.

The house was empty, with no sign of Sam or the children. Puzzled, she decided they must have gone out for a walk, and so she made herself a cup of tea and settled down in the garden. It was still just about warm enough in the sun to sit there without a coat, and she wrapped her hands round her mug and wondered where they were.

At last she heard the Mercedes pull into the drive, and Sam and the children trooped into the kitchen.

Sam waved to her, and she got up and went in.

There were three children in the kitchen: Ben and Molly and another boy of about Molly's age. Sally thought she recognised him, but what he was doing there on a Sunday afternoon Sally couldn't imagine.

They looked upset, she realised, as she took a closer look.

'What's up?' she asked Sam.

'Toby's brother's had an accident with a lawn-mower. He's gone to hospital, and we've got Toby until his parents come back.'

'Oh, dear, Toby, I am sorry,' she said softly. He began to cry, big fat tears rolling silently down his grubby cheeks, and Sally went over to him and put an arm comfortingly round his shoulders.

'Tell you what, why don't we see if we can find a packet of chocolate biscuits and a nice video, eh?'

She led him through to the sitting-room, noticing as she did so that Sam's jeans were liberally splattered with blood. She would ask for more details once they were alone, she decided.

A few minutes later Toby, still a bit wide-eyed, was tucking into chocolate animals with Molly and Ben in front of *Superman Two* and Sally was able to corner Sam in the bedroom where he was changing.

'What happened?' she asked.

He rolled his eyes. 'It was awful. The call came just after you'd left, and I knew I couldn't leave it till you'd finished, so I bundled the kids in the car and went round. Talk about carnage.'

'What had he done?'

'Tried to help his father with the lawn. He'd got the

Flymo, started it and was walking backwards and tripped. I think he's going to lose his left foot.'

'Oh, no!'

'Oh, yes. It was a dreadful mess. I just wrapped it up in clean gauze and got the ambulance immediately. They were very good with him, but he was obviously in tremendous pain, poor lad. I said we'd keep Toby till later—I guess we may have him for the night.'

Sally nodded. 'That's not a problem, he can sleep in Ben's room. Poor boy. He must have been very shocked.'

'Not as shocked as Liam.'

'Liam? I thought I recognised Toby. Liam's a friend of Ben's, I think.'

Sam nodded. 'Yes, he is. He's been here once or twice, I recognised him. Poor kid. Of course he only had light shoes on.'

'Always the way, isn't it? Nothing like that ever happens when you stand a decent chance.'

Sam tugged clean jeans up his long legs and fastened the waist, waggling it up and down. 'Look—I'm thinner.'

She smiled. 'So am I, but not because I've been working out. I feel sluggish and disgusting. I just haven't had time to eat anything proper recently.'

'How was your Mr Turner, by the way?'

She sighed. 'Your age, reasonably slim and fit-looking—you wouldn't pick him out in a crowd as the one most likely to have an MI, anyway.'

'So why did he?'

'He'd been digging. Got a bit of chest pain, stopped for a while and it went away, so he carried on. I expect he thought it was indigestion at first.'

'Easy mistake to make.' He glanced at his watch.

'What about supper? I was going to make spaghetti bolognese, but I'm not sure I feel up to another culinary defeat. Shall I get a take-away?'

She tried hard not to smile. 'Good idea. Patients can always get me on the mobile phone—we'll set it to transfer automatically.'

Nothing was ever as straightforward as it sounded, she thought half an hour later when the children were still unable to decide what they wanted.

In the end Sam ordered three Chinese meals, one lot of fish and chips and a curry for himself.

As the phone rang yet again, Sally wondered if she would actually have time to sit down and eat it while it was still hot.

Oh, well, there was always the microwave. . .

Monday morning didn't come anything like soon enough for Sally. She was in and out all night, and it seemed each time she got home there was another call just as she got into bed.

In the end she stayed in her clothes and just lay down on top of the bed, which typically ended the stream of calls.

Toby was still with them, as Liam had had to have surgery on his foot on Sunday evening and his parents had wanted to stay with him.

His father had been back with a change of clothes and his school uniform, and spent some time reassuring him about his brother, promising to collect him after school and take him to the hospital to see Liam.

Sally wondered if she would disturb him in the night, but it seemed he was exhausted by the course of events and slept like a log.

She left Sam dealing with the three of them and went

into the surgery to make up the computer notes of the patients she had seen that weekend, before her surgery started at eight-thirty.

Martin Goody came and found her, took one look at her and disappeared, returning with a cup of coffee.

'Oh, life-saver,' she murmured.

'Busy weekend?'

'Like you wouldn't believe,' she told him. 'I think I had over forty calls.'

He whistled softly. 'Wow. I think my record is forty-two.'

'Mmm. Sam said something like that. Trust me to have a mega-weekend the only one I have to do!'

Martin laughed. 'That's the way it goes, Sally. At least you can hand back to Sam at the end of the week.'

Five more days.

Suddenly it seemed terribly close—too close, almost.

'Did you want anything?'

He shrugged. 'Just to know how you'd got on. Make sure you were coping and all that. I wouldn't trust Sam to swap back in a hurry—he must be living the life of Riley at the moment.'

Sally laughed. 'Actually he's reduced to cheating. He got Dustbusters in to sort the house out, and he keeps buying take-aways!'

Martin chuckled and pushed himself up off the desk with a sigh. 'Oh, well, I suppose I'd better go and get stuck in. See you.'

He waggled his fingers and left her, and she watched him go and thought how kind he was. Sam was very lucky to have a senior partner who was so easy to get on with. Not everyone was so lucky.

Jackie came in with the stack of notes for the morning surgery, and she flicked through them, noting

with interest that old Mrs Wright was coming back to
see her. She wondered if her giddiness was worse, and
once again was assailed by doubts. Perhaps she should
have sent her to a neurologist for a check.

She was the third patient, and Sally found herself
dreading the woman's entrance into the room.

She needn't have worried. She came round the door
head first, beaming, and bustled over to the chair.

'I won't keep you, dear,' she said, 'but I just wanted
you to know I'm completely better!'

Sally was actually delighted, but pointed out to Mrs
Wright that a phone call would have done, and even
that wasn't strictly necessary.

'Oh, dear—I hope you didn't mind me coming in,
only I wanted to thank you personally.'

Sally smiled at her tolerantly. 'Of course I don't
mind—I'm really glad you're better. Thank you for
letting me know.'

She watched her go, thinking as she went that it was
a shame all consultations weren't so positive and brief.
Still, if they were, there'd be little point in her pres-
ence, so it was probably just as well!

In her break at ten-thirty she phoned the hospital to
ask after Brian Turner and Liam O'Connor, and was
told that Mr Turner had suffered a massive MI and was
on heparin, and was still not out of the woods. Such a
major heart attack at his age was not good news, of
course, and Sally wondered how his wife was taking
the news.

Liam O'Connor, on the other hand, was doing better
than Sam had expected. His foot had required very
long and tricky microsurgery, but they had managed to
save it and they were hoping he would recover almost
normally. It had required a team effort of neurology

and orthopaedics to reconstruct the foot, but they were
confident that, apart from the loss of one toe, he would
be back to normal within a few months.

Toby would be relieved, Sally knew. He had looked
quite troubled earlier that morning, and had asked if
there was any news. Poor little lad. It must have been
a horrendous shock for him. He had apparently been
standing right beside Liam when it happened, and had
grabbed the mower and pulled it off him, thus probably
saving the foot.

She went back to her surgery and called the next
patient. He was a lad of about seventeen, and one look
at him was enough to tell her why he was there.

He had possibly the worst case of acne she had ever
seen, and she had a feeling that under the very sore
rash he was blushing.

'Hi, there,' she said with a friendly smile. 'I don't
think we've met—I'm Sally Alexander. You must be
Rob Saunders.'

'That's right,' he mumbled.

'Rob, have a seat and tell me about your problem.'

He perched awkwardly on the edge of the chair. 'Its
my acne.'

'It is looking very angry and sore. Have you had any
treatment?'

He shook his head. 'My dad says zits are zits, and he
had 'em as a kid, so why am I making such a fuss, but
it hurts.'

'I'm sure it must. Anyway, acne isn't just about
spots, it's about infected spots, and you need a long
course of antibiotics to deal with acne like that. May I
have a look?'

She stood beside him and very gently ran her fingers
over the affected areas, feeling to see how deep the

cysts were. They were, as she'd thought, very deep-seated.

'Is it on your back as well?' she asked, and he nodded miserably.

'Summer's coming too, and how can I take my shirt off when I look like this?'

'May I see?' Sally asked gently, aware of the depth of his embarrassment.

He stripped off his shirt and revealed a mass of red swollen pustules all over his back. There was some scarring already, she noted, but not much. With any luck he could be treated and much of the inevitable scarring could be prevented.

'Fine—put your shirt back on, Rob. Right, I think you need to be referred to the hospital for treatment with a new drug called isotretinoin. It's a very drastic treatment, and it needs hospital supervision, but it can have marvellous results with severe acne.'

'Hospital? For zits? Dad'll die laughing.'

'Only an outpatient clinic—and whatever your father says about zits, what you have is very sore and infected skin and you need appropriate treatment.'

He looked relieved, as if someone for the first time had actually taken his suffering seriously.

'Mum says it because I eat so much junk food, like chips and stuff.'

'There is actually no evidence that junk food or greasy food or chocolate can make any difference at all,' she assured him. 'However, a healthy diet wouldn't do you any harm at all, so your mother's advice isn't entirely wrong.'

He grinned weakly. 'I hate boiled cabbage.'

'So have salad. Do you like salad?'

He nodded.

'Fruit? Eat lots of fruit and salads, and try and spend some time in the sun. It's very good for the skin, unless you have too much. But for heaven's sake make sure you don't burn! The last thing you need on top of that lot is sunburn!'

His smile widened. 'That would really be the pits,' he agreed.

'Right,' she said, getting down to basics. 'I need to take some blood from you so we can run various tests on you, and you'll need the results for the hospital clinic. At the moment the wait to see someone is about two months, but there's a lot we can do to start with. I'm going to put you on antibiotics, and you'll need a topical antibiotic cream to put on the affected areas.

'You also need to watch for things like athlete's foot, and eat live natural yoghurt every day to make sure the yeast in your gut doesn't go mad while you're on the antibiotics, but don't take it at the same time or the antibiotic won't work.'

After giving him a list of seemingly endless instructions and a card to fill in with his progress as the days went by, she let him go, armed with a ray of hope and the knowledge that someone, at least, was taking his suffering seriously.

The father was half his problem, of course. How any caring parent could make fun of a boy so miserably afflicted with acne was beyond her, and she found it made her very angry.

Presumably he'd be upset if the boy was burned and thus scarred for life, so what about acne, which could be just as damaging to the skin?

Some people, she mused as she called in her next patient, didn't deserve to be parents.

One woman who did deserve to be a parent came

home from hospital with her baby that day, and Sally went to visit her in the afternoon, even though she was off duty.

Sue Palmer was looking very well—much better than when Sally had last seen her—and lying beside her chair in a carry-cot was a tiny little doll.

'Oh, she's minute!'

Sue smiled tenderly. 'Yes, she is, but she's a real little fighter. I love her to bits.'

'I'm so glad. How are you—how's the tum?'

'Much better now. They didn't give me a bikini cut, of course, because of the hurry, but I don't care. So what if I have a scar? Look at her—don't you think she's worth it?'

Sally ran a finger gently over the downy cheek and sighed. 'You nearly lost her—I'm sorry I didn't admit you earlier.'

'What for?' Sue asked in surprise. 'I wasn't that bad—really, if you'd tried to send me in earlier I might have refused to go! I was still waiting for the contractions to start rhythmically, instead of one long ache, when the placenta came away. What is it they call it?'

'Abruptio placentae. It often is pretty abrupt, as well.'

Sue chuckled. 'Mine certainly was, good heavens. Anyway, she's fine. We've called her Sally, after you— I hope you don't mind?'

Sally's skin prickled all over, and her eyes filled. 'Oh, Sue. . .'

'Well—we reckoned if you hadn't been so thorough and warned me so much to tell you the second it got any worse, I might have just got Pete to take me to hospital, and by then she probably would have been dead.'

Sally shuddered, and laid a hand gently over the baby. 'Don't. It doesn't bear thinking about.'

'Do you want to hold her?'

Sally looked down at the tiny little scrap and her arms ached. 'It seems such a shame to wake her. . .'

'She probably won't. She sleeps like a log. Just pick her up.'

Sally slid her hands under the tiny baby and lifted her against her shoulder.

'Oh, she smells lovely—new!'

Sue grinned. 'Gorgeous, isn't it? Does it bring back memories?'

'Oh, yes—not that mine were ever this tiny.' She smoothed the soft down on the baby's head and sighed. 'Ben was almost twice this size when he was born, and Molly wasn't much smaller. They smelt the same, though—or maybe it's the hospital shampoo? I'd better put her down again before I'm tempted to rush off with her.'

She laid her carefully on the sheet and covered her again, unaware of the wistful smile on her face.

Sue wasn't unaware of it, though. 'You could always have another one,' she suggested cautiously. 'You're still young enough, surely?'

Sally shook her head. 'No—I'm free now. It was wonderful, having tiny ones, but I'm enjoying my two as they are. We can do things together now and if we had another we would be back to square one again—anyway, Sam's had a vasectomy.'

Sue nodded, then her face clouded over. 'I gather Gabby Lennard died. That was dreadful.'

'Yes—yes, it was. She had a brain haemorrhage. It could have happened at any time.'

'She was due four weeks after me—it makes me realise how lucky I am.'

'You are—we all are. It's worth remembering.'

They shared a sad smile, and then Sally took her leave.

Poor Gabby. If she had never become pregnant she might never have been troubled by the aneurism. Still, life was full of if-onlys.

One had to ignore them and get on, enjoying every day to the full.

Sally had a sudden vision of herself in ten years' time, still pushing the vacuum cleaner. Was that all she had to look forward to?

Perhaps she could do some locum work occasionally. She wouldn't want a regular commitment in another practice, and there was no room for her in Sam's.

Pity, that. It would have suited her down to the ground.

Assuming he would be agreeable, which was by no means certain.

Not that it mattered. Castles in the air, she thought with a sigh, and went home.

CHAPTER NINE

SAM greeted her with a grin. 'Good day?'

'Mercifully short,' she said drily, and he laughed and hugged her.

Just as her arms were coming round him, he slipped away and ended up on the other side of the room.

'Tea?'

She eyed him thoughtfully. 'Need to ask?'

He was wearing those jeans, she mused. The old ones that fitted him like a familiar glove—or a lover.

Her heart skipped a beat. Damn it, he was still so sexy. . .!

Settling herself at the table, she studied him as he made the tea, loving everything she saw. The way the hair grew at the back of his neck, the shape of his ears, the broad, square set of his shoulders narrowing to slim hips and neat, firm buttocks tautly encased in that wickedly familiar faded denim. And then there were those gorgeous, gorgeous legs. Strong and solid, they weren't heavy, the thigh-bones slightly rangy. Mentally she stripped the jeans off and pictured him clad only in a fine dusting of golden hair.

The image was too powerful. She shut her eyes and sighed.

'Tired?'

'Mmm,' she agreed, only too ready to keep her secret.

He put the tea down on the table in front of her.

'Here, drink this, then you can come with me to get the children.'

'Oh, I meant to tell you, they think they've managed to save Liam's foot.'

'I know—I rang, too.'

She might have known he would. He crossed his legs, the long lean muscles of his thighs clearly outlined by the jeans. 'How was Toby?' she asked, to drag her mind off the subject of his legs.

'Oh, not too bad. Very worried, and haunted by what he'd seen, but I explained that a little bit of blood can go an awfully long way. He's dying to see his brother, but at the same time I think he's also a little afraid, because the last time he saw Liam he was screaming and smothered in blood.'

Sally shuddered. 'Don't. I hope you gave our two a lecture on safety in the home.'

He laughed. 'I don't think it was necessary. I left them in the car, but they could still hear Liam. When I got back to them after the ambulance went they were white as sheets.'

'Poor kids. It was unfortunate I was already out.'

'Mmm. Still, I'm glad it was me and not you who had to deal with it.'

'I'm just as capable of being professional as you, Sam,' she told him bluntly, a little stung by what she saw as criticism.

He looked surprised. 'Well, of course you are. It was just fairly nasty. I'm glad you didn't have to see it.'

'Oh.' Mollified, she sipped her tea.

He eyed her over his mug. 'Have I told you how lovely you look with bags under your eyes?' he said gently.

'Pig.'

He smiled, a slow, lazy smile. 'You do look tired. How about a nice early night?'

It sounded wonderful. She wondered if she could talk him into giving her a massage—followed, perhaps, by a long, slow session of lovemaking. . .

She felt her cheeks heat slightly. He was still teasing her, of course—little touches every now and again, like that hug, for instance. Just when it was getting interesting, off he would go.

Well, she'd catch him one day soon, and he'd better be ready for it.

Sam watched her watching him, and sudden doubts clouded his mind. What if he couldn't please her after all? What if she'd grown so used to tuning him out that he could no longer reach her?

Fear brushed him, making the hairs stand up on his arms. He put his mug down on the table with a little smack and stood up.

'Shall we fetch the children?' he said abruptly.

Her eyes widened slightly. 'A bit early, aren't we?'

'Um—I want to get a paper from the shop first.'

'But we've got a paper—it came this morning.'

Hell. 'An evening paper,' he flannelled.

'Oh. Right.' She put down her tea, half finished, and stood up, stretching luxuriously.

Sam's gut clenched. The way her firm, pert breasts pushed against that fine jumper was enough to drive him wild. He could feel the fit of his jeans altering, and dragged his eyes away.

Damn. He didn't want her catching him turned on like a randy adolescent by the sight of her breasts— damn, there he went again, just with the thought.

He picked up his car keys and headed for the door.
'Coming?'

'Patience is a virtue,' she said, calmly following at
her own speed.

He didn't dare look, but he had a feeling that if he
did he'd catch a little smirk on her lips. He'd intended
to give her another massage that night. Frankly, he
didn't think he had the strength of will to go through a
repeat of the other night and walk away. It had nearly
killed him to say goodnight and lie there, listening to
her frustrated little noises.

There again, maybe he would try. In a masochistic
way, it was worth every second. . .

'Oh, yes, just there,' she groaned, and he dug his
fingers deeply into the tense muscles of her neck and
kneaded them firmly.

'You're incredibly tense,' he told her in surprise.

'It was a grim weekend.'

'Yes, it was. How's that now?'

'Better,' she mumbled.

He continued working for a few minutes more, his
touch slower, more sensuous. It was time to turn her
over, he thought, and his pulse quickened. He sat back
on his heels beside her.

'Better now?'

Silence greeted him. Peering over her shoulder at
her face, he saw that she was asleep.

Asleep, for God's sake!

He gave a rueful chuckle and climbed carefully off
the bed, covering her lightly.

Damned aphrodisiac oil! It had sent her to sleep!

Not so him—oh, no! Every last damn nerve-ending

had snapped to attention—and not only the nerve-endings!

Frustrated, aching with unrequited lust, he went into the bathroom and ran a hot bath, then lay in it, eye to eye with the cause of all his problems.

'Later, my friend,' he promised. 'Much later. Just hang on in there, your turn will come.'

But not nearly soon enough. He groaned and slid under the water.

Sally learned on Tuesday that Carol Bailey, the girl with the brain abscess following the infected ear, was out of danger and had been transferred from ITU to the neurology ward.

'She was lucky to survive that,' Martin said pragmatically. 'Stupid girl. It's not as if it's the first time.'

'Perhaps that's why she was so casual—because she had no reason to believe it wouldn't follow the same course?'

Martin said, 'Humph,' and updated her on Liam O'Connor. He was progressing well, and the doctors were increasingly hopeful that the surgery had been successful. He was a patient of Martin's, not Sam's, and Sally was happy to hand over his follow-up since the boy was a friend of Ben's.

She made a follow-up visit to David Jones, who was still finding his shingles painful although now rather less so. Sally reduced his medication to lower the risk of drug dependency, and was pleased to see that the infection had cleared up. In fact the crusts were almost all gone, and she could see that, provided he didn't suffer from post-herpetic neuralgia, he would be fine.

She told him so, and he was pleased to hear that he had turned the corner.

'I couldn't believe how bad it was,' he said, 'I've never known pain like it.'

Sally commiserated with him. 'It is a wretched thing. Because it's fairly common, people tend to underestimate it until they have it.'

'Not me—not any more,' he said with the first laugh Sally had seen from him in two weeks.

Pleased with his progress, she told him she wouldn't need to see him again unless he had any problems.

'Well, hopefully I won't,' he said with a smile. 'And thank you for all you've done for me. I've been a real nuisance.'

'No, you haven't. You're what we're here for,' she assured him.

It was true, she reflected as she drove away. Although she hadn't been able to halt the disease, with the antiviral drugs and the painkillers she had certainly been able to moderate its course and diminish its symptoms.

And that was what it was all about.

She would miss that aspect of the work. Miss it dreadfully. She chewed her lip. She wondered if Sam had any idea of how much she had enjoyed being back in the traces. She had needed this time to prove to herself that she was still a viable human being.

Somehow being a good mother and a good wife and a good home-maker wasn't enough.

It should have been, but it wasn't. She sighed deeply. Was there a flaw in her womanliness that she couldn't make domesticity sufficiently rewarding?

Her mind knew that wasn't true, but her heart—her heart was still having grave doubts. She wasn't happy, though. Flawed or not, she wasn't happy, and coming back to work had only served to make it worse.

Next week would be fine. There was tons to do in the garden, and she could spend time with her friends, but the week after? And the week after that?

The years that followed, yawning away into the hereafter, didn't even bear thinking about.

There was a practice meeting that evening to which she was not invited.

Sam was, of course. As one of the partners it was essential he should attend, and Sally was only a locum after all.

She looked after the children, enjoying their bath-time routine, and promised to take Ben to see Liam in hospital after the week was over. 'Perhaps after school one day next week if you haven't got too much homework,' she promised him.

'We won't, 'cause it's the end of term this Friday.'

'Really?' Sally said, stunned that the time had gone so fast. 'Is it really nearly Easter?'

He nodded. 'Can I have a Mars egg?'

'Only if you promise to eat your supper,' she threatened.

He giggled. 'It was just that one time we had a king-sized one.'

'Hmm. Once too often. Your father's much too soft with you.'

'It'll be great having you back,' Ben confided as she tucked him up. 'I mean, Dad's done his best, but he's not you.'

She smiled fondly at him and ruffled his hair. 'He hasn't had as much practice, that's all.'

'No, it's not,' he said earnestly. He struggled with his loyalty, but then the need to talk overcame his reluctance to split on his father.

'He can't cook for toffee, and he gets ever so grotty

when something goes wrong. Me 'n' Molly just hide, usually, till it's over.'

'He does love you, though,' Sally told him. 'You do know that, don't you? It's just his way.'

Ben nodded thoughtfully. 'I s'pose. It'll still be nice to have you back.'

She hugged him hard. 'It'll be nice to be back,' she told him, and it wasn't altogether a lie. In many ways it would be lovely.

She just hoped that a taste of the other side of life hadn't ruined her for the one she was stuck with.

Sam sat at the table in the practice office, and looked round him. He seemed to have been away for ever, and yet everything looked exactly the same—even that tatty poster that really ought to come down.

He didn't take it down, though. It was part of the natural order of things and quite reassuring.

Martin was there, and Steve, and Mavis, the practice manager. They covered the usual practice business, then Martin turned to Mavis and thanked her for her time.

'You may as well go now, we've covered just about everything and I don't want to keep you any later than we have to.'

Surprised, she wished them goodnight and left. Sam, too, looked surprised.

'What's going on?'

Martin tapped his pen on the table, giving it considerably more attention than such an everyday pen deserved.

'Sally.'

Sam groaned. 'What about her? Damn, I knew I

shouldn't have agreed to this idiotic idea of hers. Is it
that Palmer woman? Is she suing?

Martin looked stunned. 'Good heavens, no! Rather
the opposite, I gather. They were very taken with her,
thought she was wonderful.'

Sam felt relieved, then puzzled. 'So what is it, then?
Has she done something else?'

'No, no.' Martin soothed. 'Actually, we're all rather
taken with her. She's fitted in wonderfully well, just as
if she'd never been away. She's been a pleasure to
work with, a real pleasure. She's done everything you
would have done, the way you would have done it, and
she's been a gem. Cheerful, friendly, co-operative—
frankly, Sam, we'll miss her. Actually, that's what we
wanted to talk about.'

Sam was stunned. Delighted that Sally had fitted in
so well, disgustingly proud of her, but stunned, for all
that. He was also confused. 'Talk about what?' he
asked, his brows knitting in a frown.

Martin cleared his throat and went back to studying
his pen. 'How would you feel,' he asked eventually,
'about Sally coming back to work here part time?
About half—say, point five or point six? We can justify
the extra staffing, and frankly, Sam, we're pushed to
manage without more help. We have been for some
time, and we'd be entitled to extra funding.'

'So what are you saying?' Sam asked, groping for
understanding. 'You want to offer Sally the job?'

'That depends how you feel about working with your
wife, and how she would feel about it. I know she'll
miss it a great deal, she's said so. Whether she'd like
to work here once you're back, I don't know. I guess
that depends on how things are between you now.'

Sam was pole-axed. It was the last thing he had

expected, although he should have seen it coming. For heaven's sake, they had talked often enough about getting another part-time partner, preferably female, so it should harly come as a surprise that they wanted Sally.

'Can I think about it?' he asked them slowly. 'Sound her out, perhaps?'

'Of course,' Martin agreed, apparently relieved that he hadn't said a flat "no" outright. 'Anything you like. We won't say anything to her in the meantime, just in case you feel you couldn't work with her. The only thing is, we do really need another pair of hands, and ideally we want a woman. She might feel hurt not to have been asked if that should be the case, so I would have a damn good excuse ready or your running spikes, one or the other.'

'Of course, she may not want to do it, which would solve that problem, but we'd then have to find someone else who fitted in as well, and that could be very hard,' Steve added, looking hopelessly disappointed.

It was clear to Sam that they both wanted Sally for the job. It was equally clear that the decision was being left up to him. It was a daunting responsibility.

'I'll—um. . .' He cleared his throat and tried again. 'I'll ask her about how she feels it's gone, see if I think she'd want to go back to work. If I think she would, I'll put it to her. I know she's found full time very demanding, though.'

'What about you?' Martin asked. 'I think it's very important that you don't enter into this lightly, without thinking it through. I mean, God forbid, but what if you should get divorced in the future?'

Sam blinked. 'Sally and I aren't getting divorced,' he said.

'Stranger things have happened. I'd hate this to be the straw that broke the camel's back.'

'It might just be exactly what she needs—and what she needs, our marriage needs,' Sam said quietly. 'As I said, Sally and I aren't getting divorced—now or ever.'

As he left them, he hoped to God that he was right.

As for working with Sally, well, he'd done it before. He could probably do it again. They'd thrived on it then, before the children had come along.

There would have to be some major changes, though. Changes that both of them would have to get used to.

And then there was the problem of the children and the school holidays.

Suddenly the whole thing seemed insurmountable.

Mrs Deakin, the woman Sally had put on HRT in patch form, came to see her on Thursday and Sally hardly recognised her.

'You've had your hair done!' she said with a smile.

The smile was returned tenfold. 'I can't thank you enough for that piece of advice, or for the patches. I feel so much better!'

Sally was delighted. 'Good! I'm really pleased. Have you noticed a difference in the night sweats?'

'Oh, yes, within the first five days or so. And the flushing in the daytime, and I have so much more energy—I find it quite incredible that losing such a tiny little amount of hormone can have such a devastating impact on my well-being, but it has, and getting it back has just transformed my life—and my husband's. I've taken your advice and rediscovered the old lover, and I tell you what, it beats a new lover hands down!'

Sally laughed with her. 'Well, that's wonderful. I hope it continues to work. If not, there are all sorts of other forms of HRT we can try. In the meantime, you carry on having fun and enjoying life.'

'Oh, I will!' Mrs Deakin stood up to go, then turned back to Sally. 'Are you still going to be here? I heard a rumour that you'd swapped roles with your husband for a short time. Does that mean you won't be here any more?'

Sally nodded. 'It does, I'm afraid. Sam will, though, of course, and he'll carry on with your treatment.'

'But it won't be the same. I mean, he won't tell me to go and have my hair cut, will he?'

Sally laughed. 'No, I don't suppose he will. I can tell him to, if you like?'

She shook her head, smiling. 'No. That won't be necessary. I'm going to have it done regularly now so I don't get in that mess again. Anyway, I won't keep you. I just wanted to thank you for all your help and say goodbye. I think it's a shame you're going. You'll be missed.'

Sally swallowed a sudden lump in her throat. 'Thank you—thank you very much. I'm just glad I've been able to help you.'

Damn. Stupid sentimental fool. The door closed softly behind Mrs Deakin and Sally went to the window and stared blankly out, blinking away the tears.

Only one more day to go.

What a bleak thought.

She was just going home that night when she was hailed by Mavis.

'Letter for you, Sally. It was delivered by hand earlier this afternoon.'

She paused at reception. 'Dr Sally Alexander. That's me.' She slit the envelope and pulled out the contents.

A couple of pieces of card fell out of the folded sheet of paper to the floor, and Sally stooped to retrieve them. 'Theatre tickets? How odd.'

She unfolded the sheet of paper and stared at it in amazement.

Dear Dr Alexander,

We hope we have found the right person, but you have been difficult to track down. We wanted to thank you in some way for saving our lives the other night, because there is no doubt in our minds that if you hadn't been so brave and sensible, we would have been killed when our car exploded.

We do hope you have made a complete recovery. We both have, and have you to thank for it.

Please, therefore accept the enclosed theatre tickets for this Saturday night. We hope you are able to use them, and to join us for a complimentary meal afterwards at our restaurant 'Brooks' opposite the theatre, to give us an opportunity to thank you again in person.

Yours most sincerely,
Bernard and Louise Brook

Sally burst into tears.

Sam was totally frustrated. Everything he tried to do he made a complete carve-up of. He'd done a real meal tonight, with proper vegetables instead of frozen ones, and where had it got him?

Upside-down under the sink was where, taking the darned waste-disposal unit to bits to get the vegetable knife out.

One last thump with the wrench, and the unit was free, landing on his chest and splashing foul water in his face.

Damn and blast!

He came up, spluttering, to find Sally standing in the doorway staring at him in amazement.

'What are you gawping at?' he growled.

'Not bad, thanks. How was yours?'

'Don't get witty. I'm not in the mood,' he warned her.

She laughed. 'Darling, it's a good job you told me, I might never have noticed. Um—what are you up to?'

'What the bloody hell does it look like?' he growled. God, that water tasted disgusting.

She blinked. 'Sorry I asked.'

He sighed and sat up, wiping his mouth on his sleeve. 'I dropped the vegetable knife in the waste-disposal unit by accident.'

Her mouth made a soundless O.

He snorted. 'So, how *was* your day?'

'Wonderful, in a rather sad way. Everybody's been rather nice to me.'

He felt his insides mellow, the hard knot of irritation fading. 'Were they? Why should you be so surprised at that?'

She shrugged. 'I'm just not used to people voicing their appreciation.'

Sam felt a pang of guilt. She was right, he had taken her for granted in the past. Not any more, though.

'That's my fault,' he said quietly. 'I'm sorry.'

She lifted her shoulders again, the gesture poignant. 'Are we doing anything on Saturday night?'

Tension suddenly zinged in the air between them.

'I'm not sure,' he said slowly, the waste-disposal unit forgotten. 'Why?'

The question was cautious. He did have plans for Saturday, but tentative ones, plans that rather depended on the next twenty-four hours for their success.

She brandished something at him, little squares of white card. 'We've been given some theatre tickets for Saturday.'

'Who by?'

'Bernard and Louise Brook—the people I rescued from the car?'

'Oh—yes. How kind of them.' He wiped his hands on a rag and stood up. Theatre tickets, eh? Well, that might even fit in rather well with his plans. 'No, I can't think of any reason why we can't go.'

'They've also invited us to join them for a meal at their restaurant afterwards, on the house.'

He blinked. Even better. 'Excellent.'

'So we can go?'

'Yes—of course.'

'I'll fix a baby-sitter.'

Sam opened his mouth to tell her not to bother, and then shut it. He'd just have to find out who she'd contacted, so that he could cancel them.

No way was he telling Sally his surprise—not until tomorrow night!

He was assailed by a sudden attack of butterflies. Oh, God, what if he couldn't reach her? What if he failed hopelessly? What if he was as inept with her as he seemed to be with everything else these days?

Oh, God, surely not? A guy had to have some breaks!

* * *

Sally woke up on Friday morning with a deep sense of foreboding. It reminded her of when she was a child on the last day of the holidays, knowing that tomorrow school would start and it would all be over.

'Here — cup of tea for you.'

Well, it was the last time, so she might as well enjoy it. She struggled to a sitting position and took the mug from Sam with a murmured word of thanks.

He seemed quiet this morning, too — preoccupied. It was almost a relief when the children came in and broke the silence.

'Last day today!' Ben said delightedly. 'Then we're going to——'

There was a kerfuffle under the bedclothes, and Ben said, 'Ouch!' and then blushed.

'—be on holiday,' he finished, somewhat lamely.

Sally looked from Sam to Ben and back, and then at Molly. They all looked as guilty as sin.

'What's going on?' she asked.

'Nothing. Kids, uniform, please. Come on. Let's not be late today. Darling, why don't you go and shower?'

He took the mug firmly out of her hands and twitched the quilt off her.

With a sigh she swung her legs over the side of the bed and stretched, pulling the nightie tight. Sam's breath caught audibly, and she smiled in satisfaction as she stripped it off over her head and dropped it on the bed behind her as she headed for the shower.

Let him squirm, she thought. Do him good. If Mrs Deakin can do it, so can I.

Her morning surgery was predictably busy. With the weekend coming up and people going away on holiday, every last little ache, pain and sore throat passed through her door, or so it seemed.

She had an abscess to lance, a plaster check on a little girl who had fallen at a swimming-pool the day before and broken her arm, and a whole host of repeat prescriptions to sign and letters to get off. She wanted to leave her desk—Sam's desk, she corrected herself— absolutely clear for his return, and as the day ebbed away she rang him.

'I won't be home for lunch,' she told him. 'I'm a bit snowed-under here. I'll see you about seven.'

'Fine. You carry on,' he said, and she wasn't sure if it was her imagination or if he'd sounded relieved.

Jackie slipped out at lunchtime and brought her back a sandwich, and she ate it while she signed the repeat prescriptions and letters.

She was still in there working away when an elderly lady, tiny and very stooped, came up to the reception counter.

'Is there anybody there?' she asked weakly.

Sally immediately went round into the waiting-room. 'Hello—can I help you?'

'Oh, I hope so. I've got such a pain. . .'

She was clutching her chest in the region of her sternum, and Sally led her gently to a chair and helped her sit down. 'I haven't got an appointment. . .'

'That doesn't matter. Are you a patient here?'

She nodded. 'Yes—Dr Alexander's, I think. I don't know, I hardly ever need to see him.'

'OK. What's your name?'

'Winnie Bell—Winifred. 10 Orchard Close.'

'Got it,' Jackie called, and handed the notes to Sally.

Sally didn't want to move her, so she sat beside her and asked her a variety of questions to try and establish the source of the pain. Her spine was so badly bowed from osteoporosis that she could hardly lift her head straight, so her pain could be musculoskeletal, or gastro-oesophageal, or cardiac in origin. Her gnarled hands rested on her stick, her knuckles white, and she was obviously still in pain.

'Have you had the pain before?' Sally asked.

'Oh, yes, but never this bad.'

'When do you get it? Is it when you exert yourself, or after food, or if you bend?'

'Usually if I do too much, but often after food. I spend a lot of time in my garden—it's only small but I like to see it nice.'

'OK.' Sally fished her stethoscope out of her pocket and listened to the woman's heart, but could hear nothing untoward. It wasn't perfect, but she was no spring chicken either and one couldn't expect miracles.

'Does the pain go anywhere else—down your arm, up into your jaw?'

'Oh, my jaw, sometimes—up under here, like this.' She tilted her chin and indicated an area that was served by the same nerve as the heart.

Sally nodded. 'Do you still have the pain now?'

'Oh, yes, I do.'

Sally took a little white tablet out of her bag and held it out.

'Just pop this under your tongue for me and let it dissolve slowly, could you?'

'What is it? Heart pills? My brother had these— TNT, he used to call them. Said they blew away the pain.'

Sally smiled. 'That's right. Actually they're called GTN—glyceryl trinitrate. If it's pain from your heart, it should go in a moment.'

After about a minute the woman's breathing became less tense and she sighed. 'Oh, that's better dear. Oh, my goodness, what a relief. Like a weight's been taken off my chest.'

'Right. Good.' Sally was relieved. She didn't want to have to deal with a full-blown heart attack, and to know it was just angina eased her mind, although that was quite bad enough.

'Let's take you through to the surgery, give you a good look and see if we can provide something more long-term to help you.'

'Can you manage, Dr Alexander?' Jackie asked.

'Dr Alexander? But I thought Dr Alexander was a man—rather good-looking, if I remember.'

Sally tried to suppress her smile. 'He's my husband. We've swapped for a bit.'

'Put him to work at home, have you, dear?' Mrs Bell gave a wheezy chuckle. 'Do him good.'

'It's done me good, too. Still, he'll be back on Monday and I'll make sure I tell him all about you so he can follow you up properly, because we're going to have to keep an eye on this so you don't suffer any unnecessary pain.'

'Pity you can't stay—you're nearer my height, I can see you better. He's a bit too far up!'

Sally laughed. 'I'll tell him to sit at your feet.'

Winnie Bell chuckled again. 'I can just see that, dear. Oh, well, I'll just have to bring my periscope with me.'

Sally examined her thoroughly, doing an ECG to check her heart rhythm, and testing and inspecting almost everything. Apart from the evidence of osteoporosis and the angina, she could find remarkably little wrong.

As she helped her to dress, she said, 'You're doing very well, aren't you? How old are you, Mrs Bell?'

'Ninety-five. I'll be ninety-six in the autumn.'

Sally didn't doubt she would be. In fact, she thought it quite likely she would see the century out. 'I'll have to make sure Sam takes good care of you,' she promised.

'I'm sure you will, dear,' she said, patting Sally's arm. 'You've got a kind face—he's a lucky man. You tell him that from me.'

Sally swallowed that annoying lump again. 'I will—thank you. Now, about this pain. I think we need to give you something that will work all the time to combat this problem. I think I'm going to put you on isosorbide dinitrate twice a day to help the blood flow in your heart muscle, because your pain is due to cramp in the heart itself because it's being asked to work harder that it wants to. I'll also give you some GTN to take if you get an acute attack like just now, and you can take as many of them as you need to in a day.

'I also want to take some blood so we can check that you aren't a little bit anaemic, because that can cause angina, too.'

She took enough for a full blood count, thyroxine level and hyperlipidaemia while she was at it, then put a plaster on and labelled up the bottles carefully.

'OK? All done now, you can go and carry on with your garden. Just do something for me, though, could you? Don't work straight after a meal, and don't get carrried away and do too much at a time. I'm a keen gardener myself, and I know just how easy it is.'

They shared a smile, and Sally helped the elderly lady to the door—not that she needed any help now. She was much more sprightly than when she had come in.

The wonders of modern medicine, Sally thought, and then remembered that she wasn't going to be part of it for much longer—five hours, in fact.

She sighed and went back to her prescriptions.

CHAPTER TEN

SAM had the most frightful case of the butterflies. The table was laid, the meal—courtesy of a catering firm, because he wasn't taking any chances—was all ready to go, the house was spotless.

And Sam was terrified.

It wouldn't be as bad if so much wasn't riding on it, but he knew that their whole future together depended on how he handled the next few hours.

Always assuming, of course, that she did still love him.

He thought she did. She'd been sending out signals, either intentionally or otherwise, all damn week.

They'd been received, whatever they were, loud and clear. He sighed and stabbed his hands through his hair. What if the meal was awful?

'Just turn on the oven to two-twenty and pop the dish in for twenty minutes,' the woman had said.

Hah! Sam could wreck a dish in far less than twenty minutes. 'What about vegetables?' he'd asked.

'Here—already blanched. All you have to do is add boiling water, return them to the boil and give them three minutes.'

All. Again, hah!

He rang his mother. 'Hi, it's Sam. Kids all right?'

'Of course they are—darling, stop worrying. You're like an old hen.'

He sighed. 'I'm sorry. I guess I'm just nervous.'

'Darling, Sally loves you. It'll be fine.'

He screwed his eyes shut and pressed the bridge of his nose with his thumb and forefinger. 'I hope so.' Of course, his mother didn't know about their problems in the bedroom.

Cold sweat sprang out all over him as he thought about it. Cutting the phone call to his mother short, he poured himself a glass of wine and took it to the drawing-room.

He was mightily tempted to get smashed. That way he couldn't be expected to perform well.

Damn.

He set the glass down. He owed Sally this, and if it killed him, he'd deliver.

It might well. He couldn't remember being this nervous since his viva. Not even then, perhaps.

He glanced at his watch. A quarter to seven. He didn't know whether to suggest she had a bath first, or eat first, or just get the whole bedroom business out of the way before he tried to do the meal. At the moment he was sure food would choke him.

Perhaps he should tackle her on the subject of the practice, but he wanted a genuine reaction to him first, and to the job offer later.

He had decided that, provided they could overcome the domestic difficulties, he saw no problem with working with her. They might argue about things, but they'd have to agree to keep out of each other's way and not bring home to work and vice versa.

In many ways it would be wonderful to have her there and be able to share things with her. For years he'd shielded her, which was crazy because she was a doctor too, by all accounts an excellent one, and she would certainly have understood.

Instead, it seemed she'd resented what she had seen as his excluding her from his working life.

Crossed lines, again.

'Oh, Sally, come on, let's get this over with,' he muttered. He gave the glass of wine another longing look. Just then anaesthesia had never seemed so tempting.

Sally's last few hours at work were bitter-sweet. Martin came and perched on her desk and was so kind to her that she nearly cried.

Steve sought her out in the kitchen and said goodbye as he was off for the weekend. 'You've been great,' he said, and hugged her hard.

Even Mavis said that she would miss her.

Most of the patients, of course, were still seeing her for the first time and so she had to explain that it was only temporary and Sam would be back on Monday, and several of the women remarked that it was a shame they didn't have a woman doctor in the practice.

Sally had thought that, but although they had muttered about getting another part-time partner in the past, nothing had ever come of it and she didn't suppose anything ever would.

Silly, really, because they were hopelessly overstretched as it was.

Finally, Sam's desk was cleared and there was nothing left to do. She sat behind it, her hands pressed to the cool wood, and pretended it was still her desk and was going to be for the next umpteen years.

It was a nice idea while it lasted.

She couldn't stall any longer. The kids would be waiting up for her, and Sam would have tried to cook something and would be hurt if she was late.

Everything had an up-side, she thought with a smile. Once they'd swapped back they could all start enjoying their food again. Poor Sam wasn't a cook.

She loved him, though. She knew that now. It was time to tell him.

Pushing back the chair, she stood up and left the room without a backward glance.

Here she was. Right. Deep breaths, calm, nice and steady.

He wiped his palms on the sides of his trousers and swallowed.

A car door slammed, the garage door rumbled down and crashed home, and then she was in the kitchen.

'Hi.'

She smiled. 'Hi.'

'Everything OK?'

Apart from not wanting to leave the practice? 'Yes, everything's fine. I've left your desk tidy.'

'Thanks. Um—why don't you go and have a bath while I finish the supper?' he suggested, the butterflies turning to miniature drills boring away at his insides.

She gave him a funny look. 'OK. How long have I got?'

'I'll give you ten minutes' warning, all right?'

She smiled. 'OK. Thanks. Where are the kids, by the way?'

'My parents.'

'Oh.' Something flickered in her eyes, but he was too agitated to work out what it was.

He checked the table, wiped down the worktops yet again, turned on the oven to heat and then, after a few more minutes of procrastination, he put the dish in the oven.

Vegetables, now—in fifteen minutes. He set the timer, and after ten nerve-racking minutes he went upstairs and tapped on the bathroom door.

Sally opened it, already out and dried.

She was also totally, beautifully, naked.

His heart jerked in his chest. 'Um—supper's in ten minutes,' he said gruffly, and turned on his heel.

'Sam?'

He stopped. 'Yes?'

'Make love to me.'

He felt as if he'd been punched. Slowly, just in case it was only a dream, he turned. 'What?'

She smiled, a knowing smile, a woman's smile, confident and devastating.

'You heard.'

'But. . .supper. . .'

'Please.'

He was undone. Slowly, because he'd forgotten how to do it, he drew in a breath.

Her hand came up to him and he reached out and took it, letting her lead him to the bed.

'I was going to light scented candles and give you a massage with that oil——'

'I don't need that, Sam,' she whispered. 'All I need is you.'

His heart nearly stopped. His eyes did something damn funny, too, but he blinked and they cleared.

He let himself look at her, and it nearly finished him. 'You're beautiful,' he said hoarsely.

'No. I'm just me.'

'You're beautiful,' he repeated.

She reached up and started undoing the buttons of his shirt, and he thought his skin would catch fire where her fingers touched it.

She tugged the shirt out of his trousers and slid her hands round his sides, her palms cool against his heated skin.

'You feel wonderful,' she murmured into his chest. 'I've missed you.'

'I've missed you, too,' he said raggedly. 'You can't know how much.'

'Oh, I do. Believe me.'

She slid the shirt down over his arms so that they were trapped behind his back, and then turned her attention to his belt buckle. He sucked in his breath and her fingers slid over the waistband, teasing the skin of his abdomen.

He yanked his arms free, pinging one of the buttons off, but he didn't care. He didn't care if he'd ripped the whole sleeve out.

He detached her hands from his waist and eased her up against him, sighing as her soft breasts pillowed against his chest.

'Oh, you feel so good,' he murmured. He tilted her head back with one finger and brought his mouth down over hers. It opened like a flower and he used his tongue to coax it further still.

She gasped and arched against him, and he growled in satisfaction and plunged his tongue deeper, thrusting it rhythmically into the velvet depths of her mouth.

She squirmed against him, little noises coming from her throat, and he lifted her and laid her on the bed without once breaking the kiss.

He came down beside her, their lips still meshed, and her hands found the zip of his trousers and slid it down, darting inside to circle him gently.

He gasped and shackled her wrist, pulling her hand away.

'No, Sally, for God's sake. Take it steady.'

'I don't want to. I want you now.'

'No.'

There was no way he was hurrying her this time. He fastened both her wrists together with one large hand and held them above her head.

Her eyes widened in surprise. 'What are you doing?'

'Making love to you. That's what you wanted, isn't it?'

His hand slid down her throat, over her collarbones, splaying across her breasts. Her nipples peaked and she made a tiny noise and bucked.

He teased them, drawing it out until she was like a bowstring, then his hand slid lower, drifting past the soft curls and stroking the fine skin of her thighs.

'Sam, please,' she begged breathlessly.

'All in good time.'

He kissed her again while his hand found her, testing her readiness.

He nearly lost it, just doing that.

Oh, God, don't let me blow it now, he thought.

He released her and shucked off the rest of his clothes, then turned back to her.

'No faking,' he said quietly.

She met his eyes, her own deep pools of need.

'No faking,' she vowed.

'I want every last damn scream,' he told her. His mouth found hers again, plundering it while his hand sought out her most vulnerable secret.

He felt her sob, her body arching, then he covered her, thinking of anything—the garden, the supper— oh, hell, the supper. In the distance he could hear the timer on the cooker, and he tried to focus on it, picture the charred contents—anything but listen to Sally as he entered her slowly, burying himself deep inside her. . .

A huge groan tore itself from his throat and he dropped his head against her shoulder.

'Steady,' he pleaded.

'No—no, Sam, please, now!'

He was lost. He couldn't have held back then for anyone, not with her gentle plea ringing in his ears.

'I love you,' she whispered, and then he could feel the convulsions start deep within her.

He shuddered, his body pulsing, and clinging to her, he held her tight as the wild storm raged through them.

'Wow.'

She watched as he cracked an eye open and looked at her, sprawled across his chest. He looked rumpled and sexy, and she loved him. She needed to say so again.

'I do love you, Sam.'

'At the moment. You'll go off me soon.'

'Why?' She lifted her head. 'Sam, what's that smell?'

'That's the reason you aren't going to love me in a minute.'

'Supper?'

He nodded. 'It was supposed to have twenty minutes. That was nearly an hour ago.'

'Oh. I still love you.'

He looked at her and his eyes filled. 'I love you, too,' he said, his voice choked. 'I've missed you. It's been years since we've made love like that.'

She smoothed his hair back off his brow and wriggled up his chest to kiss him.

'I'm sorry I faked before. I should have made you talk to me. It was a dreadful thing to do.'

'It must have been awful for you.'

'It was—I felt so lonely, as if I was outside myself watching. We just seemed to have lost so much.'

He wrapped his arms round her tightly and held her close. She could feel his heart beating beneath her ear, and it suddenly seemed terribly important that everything should be all right between them again.

'We will be OK, won't we, Sam?' she asked him softly, suddenly afraid that she might have killed his love.

'I hope so. I'm sorry I let you feel used,' he said gruffly, his voice a deep rumble under her ear. 'I didn't mean to. I was always very conscious of how much you did for us all, but until we swapped I didn't really have any idea of just what was involved. I mean, I knew your role was important, but I didn't realise quite how much there was to do or how demanding it could be. I'm afraid I didn't do it nearly as well as you did my job.'

She laughed softly. 'It's just practice. If you'd done it for years, like I did medicine before I gave up, it would be different.'

'Hell, Sally, we're talking about housework, not neurosurgery! How difficult can it get?'

She propped herself and met his rueful eyes. 'I don't know, darling. You tell me.'

He snorted and dropped his head back. 'Impossibly difficult. I'd better go and turn that oven off and dispose of the remains of our supper.'

She shifted slightly to let him go, then watched as he pulled on his dressing-gown.

'I'll come too. We'll make an omelette or something and have a glass of wine.'

He gave a short, humourless laugh. 'If you had any

idea of the lengths I went to over this meal, you'd never let me live it down.'

She slid off the bed. 'What was it?'

'*Filet de boeuf en croûte.*'

She blinked in amazement. 'Really?'

'Really.'

They went downstairs and she watched with interest as he removed the charred mess from the oven.

'I don't suppose the meat inside is worth fishing out?' he said hopefully.

She peered at it. 'No, I don't suppose so. Was it Delia's recipe?'

'Um . . .' He scraped the mess into the sink and turned on the waste-disposal unit.

'I can't hear you.'

He switched it off. The back of his neck was red. 'I said, I got a catering firm to deliver it, all ready to put in the oven.'

She didn't have the heart to tease him this time. Instead she looked regretfully into the empty sink.

'Oh, well. Shall I make the omlettes?'

'We need to talk,' he said later, as they lay curled up together on the settee in the little sitting-room.

His fingers were plucking at the piping on the arm, and he obviously had something on his mind.

'Do you want to start?' she asked.

He shrugged, his big shoulder shifting under her cheek, and she moved away slightly so that she could watch his face. He was quite good with his voice, but his eyes gave him away every time.

'Go on, then. You first.'

His fingers caught hers and twined around them, hanging on.

'I love you,' he said finally. 'I want you to know that, because it's fundamental. Nothing else is as important as that.'

She squeezed his hand encouragingly. 'Good. Because I feel the same.'

'Nevertheless, you haven't been happy, and at least partly that's been my fault.'

'And mine.'

'I've neglected your needs,' he ploughed on, ignoring her, 'and that's unforgivable.'

'I've forgiven you. I'm hardly whiter than white——'

'I didn't listen to you. When things got tough, I made love to you because it was the quickest and easiest way to put the smile back on your face, and I needed you to smile. I need to make you happy, Sally. If I can't do that, I might as well go out and shoot myself.'

'Don't.' She wriggled closer again, wrapping her arms round his big chest and hanging on. 'It isn't you that makes me unhappy. I'm just dissatisfied with my lot, and when I think how lucky I am, I'm disgusted with myself.'

'But are you lucky? Really? As you said yourself, by an accident of biology you're stuck with the cooking and the cleaning and the taxi service for the kids, and I know you enjoy the garden, but the housework? Really?'

She laughed softly. 'No, you're right. I hate the housework and the washing. The garden I love, and I need to spend time with the children because I adore them and they're so funny they make everything seem right, but the house I could set fire to any day of the week without turning a hair.'

'I don't think that's a very wonderful idea,' he said

cautiously. 'Still, if you didn't have to do the house-work, what would you like to do with that time? Really, honestly?'

'Really? Honestly? I'd like to go back to work.'

'With me?'

She laughed. 'Ideally, yes. I know it won't happen, though. You've all talked about it, but that's as far as it will ever go, and there's no way Martin and Steve would wear you creating a job just for me. Maybe there's another practice, though.'

Sam traced the line of her nose with a blunt finger. 'What if there didn't need to be another practice? What if there genuinely was a part-time job at the practice?'

'Well, it would be marvellous, but I won't hold my breath.'

'What about the kids, though, in the holidays? Have you thought of that?'

She sighed and wriggled her fingers through the front of his dressing-gown, toying idly with the soft curls on his chest. 'Mmm. I don't know. I suppose they're old enough now, but I would still worry.'

'We could always have an au pair.'

She tweaked a hair out. 'Forget it. You're mine!'

He laughed ruefully and pulled her hand out of his dressing-gown, trapping it in his hand. 'I'm serious. There's the room above the garage. We've often talked about putting in a staircase instead of the ladder and turning it into a little flat. Perhaps we could convert it into a bed-sitting-room with a bathroom. That way we'd still have our privacy, because there's no way I'm going to sacrifice being able to wander round my own home in the nude if I want to. And you could go back to work then, either part time or full time, if you wanted to.'

She sat up and searched his face. 'You're serious, aren't you?'

He nodded.

'Well, don't you think it would be an idea to approach Martin and Steve before you start taking on a new partner without their knowledge or consent?'

He rubbed his chin. 'Actually, they approached me.'

'They did? When?'

'The practice meeting on Tuesday.'

'The one I wasn't invited to?'

He grinned. 'That's the one.'

She frowned. 'So what did they say?'

Sam smiled. 'You want to hear it? It'll make you blush.'

She blushed.

'See? I told you.'

'Idiot.' She thumped him gently and snuggled back to his chest. 'So, what did they say?'

He told her, and she felt the heat mount her cheeks.

'They said all that?'

'They did.'

'Oh.' She fell silent.

'I was very proud of you, Sally,' he said, his voice vibrant with sincerity. 'I've never loved you so much as I did at that moment.'

'Oh, Sam. . .' She reached up and cradled his cheek, turning his face to her kiss.

'Sally?'

'Mmm?'

'Do you want to think about it?'

She shook her head. 'No. If they want me that badly, who am I to disappoint them?'

'What about the kids?'

'What about them? They're getting older now.

They'll have to accept that I, too, have needs. I've denied them long enough. It's taken me a long time to reach out and grasp what ought to be mine. I'm sure they'll accept it.'

'And if they don't?'

She sighed. 'Then I won't do it yet. But I will do it, Sam. I need to, preferably now, but later if necessary. And I won't let myself be put on the back-burner out of sight any more. It doesn't do any of us any good.'

'No.' He stood up and pulled her to her feet.

'What are you doing?'

'Taking you to bed. We've got a lot of catching up to do.'

'Oh.' She let him lead her by the hand, up the stairs and into the bedroom, then he laid her down on the bed and made love to her slowly, thoroughly, giving every inch of skin his undivided attention until she was almost sobbing with need.

Then, his face sharply etched with desire, he eased over her and gave himself to her.

'That feels so good,' she whispered. Her hands slid over his shoulders, tunnelling up into his hair and pulling him down towards her.

As their lips met, she whispered, 'Let rip, Sam. I need you. Let's see how fit you really are.'

He hesitated for a second, then levered himself up and peered down at her, his wickedly sexy eyes gleaming. 'Is that a challenge?'

She smiled slowly. 'If you like.'

'I like.'

He started gently, gradually building the rhythm until she thought she would die. Again and again he took her to the brink and then eased back, letting her passion subside, tormenting her.

Then finally he didn't stop and she felt the ripples start, heard herself cry out, reaching for him, mindlessly sobbing and holding him as he shuddered against her, his body slaked at last.

'Oh, my,' she whispered breathlessly. 'Oh, Sam, that was. . .'

She trailed to a halt, unable to speak.

He levered himself up and looked down at her. 'Satisfied?' he asked wryly.

'Oh, yes. . .'

'Thank God,' he muttered, and collapsed against her. . .

They made love again that night, and off and on through the following day.

On Saturday evening they went to the theatre and saw a visiting team of players presenting a wickedly funny Alan Ayckbourn play, and then afterwards they walked across the town square to Brooks'.

As they went in, a woman Sally recognised as Louise Brook crossed the room to her and clasped her hands.

'Dr Alexander! You came.'

'Sally, please. And this is my husband, Sam. Sam, this is Louise Brook.'

'Pleased to meet you—and I'm very glad you're in such good shape!'

Louise laughed. 'Oh, me too! If it hadn't been for Sally. . .' She broke off with a shudder, and a shadow passed over her face. 'Still,' she said, forcing a bright smile, 'every cloud has a silver lining. We've got a new car now.'

'And we've had a wonderful evening at the theatre. Thank you both very much indeed.'

'Oh, our pleasure. Come on, I've saved us a table.'

She led them to the back of the restaurant and seated them, then went to find Bernard.

Sam looked round curiously. 'It's nice here. We ought to come again another time.'

'When it's your turn to cook, perhaps?'

He chuckled. 'I think the redistribution of household tasks ought to exclude cooking and washing. I don't seem to have a gift for them.'

Sally couldn't stop the laugh. 'No, somehow I don't think you do. Or gardening, although you're quite good at digging and cutting the grass. Perhaps I'll let you carry on with that.'

'You're so kind.'

Bernard and Louise joined them then, and after another round of introductions Bernard passed them the menu. 'I don't know what you fancy,' he said, 'but the *filet de boeuf en croûte* is very good tonight.'

Sam laughed out loud, and Sally bit her lips.

The Brooks looked at them in surprise.

'Sorry,' Sam said with an engaging grin. 'It's just that I wanted to impress Sally last night, so I got a firm of caterers to make me one.'

'Well, have something else, by all means.'

Sam's smile widened. 'Oh, no. I'm really looking forward to it. We didn't get to eat it last night. I put it in the oven and we got—um—sidetracked,' he said, faint colour running up his neck.

He floundered to a halt and Louise chuckled. 'How wonderful. I shall have to try cooking it for Bernard.'

They smiled at each other across the table, and Sally looked up and winked at Sam.

A wine waiter brought a bottle of champagne to the table and eased the cork out, then filled their glasses.

Bernard raised his glass. 'To Sally,' he said. 'We owe you more than we can ever say.'

'Hear, hear,' Sam said softly.

Sally's eyes filled. 'You are silly,' she said with a little laugh.

'Happy birthday,' Sam said to her, tipping his glass to her.

'Oh, is it your birthday,?' Louise asked.

Sam laughed. 'No. Not any more. I messed that up, too. Still, I think I may have sidetracked my way out of trouble for now.'

He and Sally shared a smile of understanding.

'You'll do,' she said laughingly, but she meant it.

The laughter left Sam's eyes, to be replaced by a love no one could mistake. 'Thank you,' he said softly. 'I'll hold you to that.'

She smiled her love. 'Please do. . .'

GET 4 BOOKS
AND A MYSTERY GIFT

Return this coupon and we'll send you 4 Love on Call novels and a mystery gift absolutely FREE! We'll even pay the postage and packing for you.

We're making you this offer to introduce you to the benefits of Reader Service: FREE home delivery of brand-new Love on Call novels, at least a month before they are available in the shops, FREE gifts and a monthly Newsletter packed with information.

Accepting these FREE books and gift places you under no obligation to buy, you may cancel at any time, even after receiving just your free shipment. Simply complete the coupon below and send it to:

HARLEQUIN MILLS & BOON, FREEPOST, PO BOX 70, CROYDON, CR9 9EL.

No stamp needed

Yes, please send me 4 free Love on Call novels and a mystery gift. I understand that unless you hear from me, I will receive 4 superb new titles every month for just £1.99* each postage and packing free. I am under no obligation to purchase any books and I may cancel or suspend my subscription at any time, but the free books and gifts will be mine to keep in any case. (I am over 18 years of age)

1EP5D

Ms/Mrs/Miss/Mr _____

Address _____

_____

_____

_____ Postcode _____

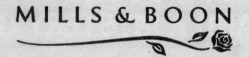

MILLS & BOON

LOVE CALL

The books for enjoyment this month are:

TAKEN FOR GRANTED	Caroline Anderson
HELL ON WHEELS	Josie Metcalfe
LAURA'S NURSE	Elisabeth Scott
VET IN DEMAND	Carol Wood

Treats in store!

Watch next month for the following absorbing stories:

IMPOSSIBLE SECRET	Margaret Barker
A PRACTICE MADE PERFECT	Jean Evans
WEDDING SONG	Rebecca Lang
THE DECIDING FACTOR	Laura MacDonald